# COPYRIGHT

Strong Enough
Copyright © 2013 Cardeno C.
Issued by: The Romance Authors, LLC, October, 2015
http://www.theromanceauthors.com

Print ISBN: 978-1-942184-43-0

Editor: Jae Ashley
Interior Book Design: Kelly Shorten
Cover Artist: Jay Aheer

This book is a work of fiction. While references may be made to actual places or events, the names, characters, incidents, and locations are from the author's imagination and are not a resemblance to persons, living or dead, businesses, or events. Any similarity is coincidental.

# REVIEWS

*A Shot At Forgiveness:* This was smufftastic fun as most CC novels and novellas are, and as such I enjoyed reading it.

— *My Fiction Nook*

*Home Again:* Home Again is a beautiful, well-written, love story

— *Redz World*

*In Your Eyes*: I adored this story. It's sweet but also has some emotional moments that really grabbed my heart.

— *The Blogger Girls*

*McFarland's Farm*: Cardeno C is quickly becoming one of my favourite m/m romance authors, especially for a quick, sweet romance

— *BJ's Book Blog*

*Perfect Imperfections*: Perfect Imperfections has a little bit of everything and is sure to be another hit for Cardeno C.

— *Night Owl Reviews*

*Strange Bedfellows*: As with all of this author's work, Strange Bedfellows is very well-written and has a strong storyline with plenty of angst, sweetness and romance to keep even the pickiest reader highly satisfied.

— *Top 2 Bottom Reviews*

*The One Who Saves Me*: Positively phenomenal!

— *The Romance Reviews*

# DEDICATION

*To the readers who love Emilio and Spencer: Thank you!*

# CHAPTER 1

"AHEM. WHAT are you doing?"

Spencer Derdinger jumped away from his office window at the unexpected sound of a voice behind him.

"Nothing!" he shouted defensively as he turned toward the door to see Maria Lee, his colleague and friend, watching him with a smirk on her face. The wooden blinds clanked loudly against the window, making Spencer flinch.

Maria raised one eyebrow, slowly walked over to the window, placed a perfectly manicured finger on one slat, and pulled it down.

"When did you turn into such a cliché?" she asked without looking away from the window.

"I don't know what you mean." Spencer skittered over to his desk and started stacking the randomly strewn-about papers into equally random piles.

After turning around, walking over to an empty chair, and sitting down with her thin ankles crossed, Maria flipped her hair back over her shoulder and said, "Spencer, please don't insult my intelligence by pretending you weren't staring out the window and drooling over the men working on the new addition to the math building."

Spencer blushed and started rearranging the papers. "Well, technically, the cliché would be construction workers checking out women walking by, not men checking out construction workers from the privacy of their offices. So you see? I wasn't being a cliché."

"Fine," Maria said. "It was an inverse cliché."

"Is that a real thing?" Spencer asked, furrowing his brow.

Maria crossed her slender legs, causing her skirt to move up her thigh. "I have a doctorate in applied mathematics, not English, same as you. I have no idea whether it's real or not. Now quit deflecting and tell me which of those men caught your eye."

"Did you wear that outfit to class?" Spencer asked as he looked his colleague up and down.

"Why, yes, I did." Maria tilted one corner of her mouth up and tugged on the bottom of her tight sweater, causing the V-neck top to dip low enough to show impressive cleavage.

"What did you teach this morning?" he asked.

"Introductory Algebra," she answered with a glint in her eyes.

Spencer didn't bother holding back his laugh. "How many football players are in the class?"

"Oh, I don't know." Maria held her hand up and inspected her long nails. "I'd say at least half the team."

Spencer snorted. "You are evil."

"I'm strategic," she corrected as she raised her eyes to

meet his.

"You tortured a bunch of eighteen-year-olds on the off chance that they'll talk about you in front of their coach."

"Like I said," Maria drawled. "Strategic. And, honey, after the number of times I turned around and stretched, there is no *off chance* about it. I can guarantee you those boys *will* talk about me in front of Thom. But that's enough about me. Tell me which of the builder babes has you all hot and bothered."

There was no way Spencer would give Maria any more ammunition than she already had, so he said, "I have no idea what you're talking about."

Maria crossed her arms over her chest, pushing her breasts up and halfway out the top of her sweater. "Don't be coy, Spencer."

Spencer crossed his arms over his significantly less endowed chest and raised his eyebrows. "I'm not an eighteen-year-old straight boy, Maria." He tilted his chin toward Maria's breasts meaningfully. "Those don't hypnotize me."

"Fine." Maria humphed. "Don't tell me which one you're into. I'll figure it out on my own."

Fear trickled up Spencer's spine at those words. Maria was sharp, shameless, and stunning. When she set her sights on something, she succeeded every single time. Thom Bramfield, the head coach of the football team, didn't know it yet, but he didn't stand a chance against her advances. Spencer, on the other hand, knew enough to realize he had to protect himself from Maria's schemes.

"There's nothing to figure out," he said in a rush. Then he forced himself to take a breath and calm down. Maria would recognize his panic otherwise. And if she smelled blood, she'd know she was on the right trail and Spencer would never be able to shake her from her newest mission. All hope would be lost. "I mean, fine, I was looking at the men working outside," he conceded. "They're attractive and muscular, and there's no crime in looking. End of story. There's nothing to figure out here."

For the first time since she'd walked into his office, Maria's expression softened. She now looked genuinely concerned rather than calculating. "Spencer, since you and Peter broke up, I haven't seen you take an interest in any man. And even before then, I have never known your interests to be purely carnal. You've been looking out that window every day for two weeks. Those men out there are attractive, but not more attractive than lots of guys you can find online, wearing less clothing." She leaned forward and took in a deep breath before continuing. "You'll need to take a chance sometime, honey. You can't live your life holed up in that little house all alone."

Saying he and Peter broke up made it all sound so civil, like they'd amicably decided to part ways over drinks one day. Which, in a way, was true. Spencer had heard from a friend that Peter had left a bar with another man...after spending most of the night with his tongue down the man's throat.

Wanting to give his boyfriend the benefit of the doubt, Spencer had brought the topic up calmly. Then he spent twenty minutes at a little table in the coffee shop around the corner from his house, mute with shock, mug of cooling liquid between both palms, while Peter cheerfully admitted to sleeping around and then explained the things lacking in their eighteen-month relationship. All of which, according to Peter, sat squarely on Spencer's shoulders. Then Peter said they should keep in touch, brushed some crumbs off his pants, got up from his seat, and walked out the door.

Given those details, Spencer would classify the ending of his last relationship as an unequivocal dumping rather than a breakup. But he didn't want to sound pathetic, so he swallowed down that clarification and instead tried to look affronted as he said, "My house is just over eighteen hundred square feet. That's not little for a historic neighborhood."

"Fine," Maria said with a roll of her eyes. "I'll let this go."

Spencer sighed in relief. "Thank you."

"For now," she added, boring her dark-eyed gaze into him. "I'll let it go for now. But at some point you're going to have to get back on that horse."

Maria meant well, but she didn't understand. He was thirty-eight, which was considered past his prime on the bar circuit, not that he'd ever felt comfortable in bars. At five foot nine and barely shy of one hundred sixty pounds, he was average height and average weight. Add in brown eyes and brown hair, with a little bit of gray around the temples, and Spencer knew he wasn't somebody who turned heads when he walked down the street. And, as his ex had helpfully pointed out, if by some miracle he managed to get a guy to notice him, he was far too dull to keep the guy's attention for long.

"I've never ridden a horse," he mumbled, trying once again to deflect.

"I haven't either," Maria said thoughtfully. "Though I have a feeling Thom Bramfield is hung like one, so if all goes as planned, I'll be saying giddyup and bouncing away this weekend."

"Oh Lord." Spencer cringed and shook his head. "I *so* did not need that visual."

"My girls are completely lost on you," Maria said as she cupped and squeezed her breasts. Then she shrugged and said, "Oh, well. I've got plenty of admirers."

"You're a member of Mensa," Spencer said. "You can't say things like that!"

Maria took a deep breath and looked at him sympathetically. "Sure I can. There's nothing that says being intelligent precludes being sexy or fun or quirky or anything else. I can excel at statistical theories, make crass jokes, and look fabulous. All at the same time. They are not mutually exclusive." She got up, straightened her skirt, then looked meaningfully at Spencer. "Nobody can put me in a box except myself." She waltzed over to the door, turned the knob, and looked back over her shoulder. "The same is true for you,

Spencer," she said, and then she walked out of the room.

EMILIO SANCHEZ saw the blinds on the second floor office of the University of Nevada, Las Vegas math building flick shut and knew the sexy man with chinos in every shade of brown and a lifetime supply of sweater-vests was no longer watching them. He had first seen the professor two weeks earlier, when his brother called him in to take a look at the electrical panel in the building they were adding on to. When he'd answered Raul's call that day, he had expected to stop by for a few minutes and figure out the best way to move the existing panel, which was currently located on an exterior wall that would soon become interior. But then he'd locked gazes with that man and all his plans changed.

Brown eyes with specks of gold were what he noticed first. Unfortunately, he didn't get a chance to look for long before the man lowered his gaze as a red heat traveled up his neck to his cheeks. Then he scurried into the building.

Shy. The stranger was shy. And Emilio thought it was utterly charming. So he'd found a reason to stay on at the construction site, hoping he'd be able to meet the intriguing stranger.

"Yo, bro, you sure you want to stick around here?" Raul asked, diverting Emilio's attention from the now empty window. "We won't need to start the wiring for another few weeks, and I can get one of the carpenters over to work on the framing."

Sanchez Construction had started out as a family business, and though they were now big enough to require hiring outside the bloodline, his father, mother, sister, and three brothers were still the heartbeat of the company. Being raised on construction sites had made each of them a jack-of-all-trades, but they definitely had individual strong suits. Emilio was the youngest of the bunch at twenty-two, and the only licensed electrician. He figured that'd always be his specialty, even after he took the general contractor exam the following year. But that didn't mean he wasn't a damn fine carpenter as well.

"Nah, I don't mind." Emilio pushed the front of his thick black hair back and settled his gaze on his brother. "My side work is all dried up right now, and I checked on the other job sites this morning."

It was a true statement, but he could find another project in a heartbeat if he let his buddies know he had free time. Since the day he finished high school, Emilio had worked for the family business during the day, which usually started at six in the morning and ended at two in the afternoon, and then taken on small side jobs after hours. At first he'd done favors for friends or relatives who needed assistance with home improvements. But over the years, Emilio found he liked the diversity in the work—commercial projects for the family company during the day, fixing residential messes made by weekend warriors during the evening—plus he appreciated the extra money it put in his pocket.

A couple hours later, Raul said, "Hey, *hermanito*, we already went long and it's Friday, so we're wrapping up now. We're heading over to Joe's Pub for a couple of beers."

Emilio finished shooting a few more nails into the support beam he had put up and then climbed down the ladder. He stepped outside the partially framed space and glanced up at the sexy professor's window for what had to be the hundredth time that day. It looked dark. Though he had concentrated on his work, something he learned early in life was important when handling power tools, Emilio had kept watch for the guy he'd been hoping to meet but hadn't caught sight of him. That meant Emilio wasn't as observant as he thought...or the guy had left in a different direction. Either way, his plan for the night was thwarted.

"I'll skip it tonight," he said with a sigh, unable to keep the disappointment out of his voice. He'd been half-hard a good portion of the day imagining what he could do to the professor once he got him alone. Not being able to realize those fantasies left him frustrated.

"You gotta come, Emilio," Bruce Simms, one of their newer employees said as he walked over to where Emilio was packing up his tools.

Bruce was a nice guy and a hard worker, so Emilio found a smile for him as he finished loading up his gear. "Thanks,

man, but I don't think I'll be very good company tonight." He
stood and hefted up his tool chest. "Maybe next time, yeah?"

"No!" Bruce practically shouted. "It's gotta be tonight."

That was an odd reaction. Emilio raised both eyebrows
in surprise and said, "Uh, you got something you want to tell
me?"

"No. Yes." Bruce sighed and scratched at his cheek.
"Fuck," he groaned. "Okay, here's the deal. My wife's sister
saw you when you dropped me off at the house last week.
You know, when my truck was in the shop?"

Bruce paused and looked at Emilio meaningfully, so he
nodded and said, "Yeah?"

"Well, she wants to meet you, so my wife told her I'd set
it up without it looking like a setup. She's gonna happen to be
at the bar today and then she'll see me walk in and come say
hello and then I'm supposed to introduce you and..." Bruce
sighed deeply and scratched his temple, the conversation
seemingly making him itchy with discomfort. "Fuck, man,
you get the idea."

Yeah, he got the idea, which was why he now wanted to
go to the bar even less. Making polite conversation with some
guys from work seemed like too much right then. Fending off
advances from a coworker's sister-in-law was unbearable.

"Like I said, thanks for the offer, man, but I'm not up for
it tonight."

He gave Bruce a friendly punch to the shoulder and
started walking away.

"Wait, Emilio, I have a picture of her on my phone."
Bruce clasped Emilio's shoulder, trying to halt his escape.
"Don't you at least want to see what she looks like before you
say no?"

"You do understand how weird this is, right?" Emilio
asked as he turned back around to look at Bruce.

"Oh, yeah, I get it. But she's my wife's sister, and if I do
this, I'll be getting lucky for weeks. Plus, I think you two will
really hit it off. I think she's exactly your type."

How this man thought he knew Emilio's type was
anybody's guess, but he was dead wrong.

Raul must have heard the last part of the conversation,
because he started chuckling. "Boy, are you barking up the
wrong tree," he said to Bruce.

"What do you mean?" Bruce asked as he furrowed his
brow.

Emilio had come out at age eighteen. Living within a
few miles of where he grew up and where his siblings still
lived meant secrets never lasted long. He was done with high
school and had enough skills to get a job working for any
construction company in town if the shit hit the fan worse
than he expected with his family. Plus, he had an older cousin
who had been out for as long as Emilio could remember.

He had seen his cousin Asher a handful of times at
family gatherings, and nobody had ever given the big man
a hard time. Of course, harassing a person with Asher's
temperament was asking for a permanent limp, but Emilio

never even heard people bad-talk him when he went home to California. So he figured his family would probably be fine and coming right out with the information would be better than trying to hide.

The resulting drama was short-lived; once the initial shock wore off, everyone went back to living their lives. After that, Emilio figured he was out. Done and done. But in the four years since, he had realized that he'd never really be done, that coming out was an ongoing process.

There was always someone new at work or someone dating one of his relatives or someone showing up at his weekend pickup soccer games, and small talk often included seemingly innocuous questions about his personal life, like whether he was married. Emilio wasn't ashamed of being gay, but sometimes it was exhausting to have to come out yet again, and he'd find himself analyzing whether ignoring certain questions or diverting conversations away from certain topics was easier than making the "I'm gay" speech.

Now was one of those times. It had been a long week and he was in no mood for conversation. But with a setup looming and his brother teasing, Emilio had to say something.

"He means," Emilio said as he glared at his brother, "that I'm sure your wife's sister is nice and pretty and all, but she's not my type."

"Oh." Bruce seemed to deflate, and then he squinted and got tense once again, seemingly offended by Emilio's explanation. "Why isn't she your type? She looks a lot like my wife. Are you saying Sue ain't pretty?"

Well, diversion tactics weren't going to help. He might as well come out with the truth, field any annoying questions, and then go home, where he could drink a six-pack in relative peace. *Relative* because he had three roommates, which meant quiet was a rare indulgence to be savored. On a weekend night, though, he figured his chances were better than average because his roommates would probably be out getting laid or getting drunk or both.

"No, I'm not saying that at all. I'm gay, so no matter how pretty your sister-in-law is, she isn't my type," Emilio said matter-of-factly, hoping that would be the end of the conversation. He wanted to go home and relax after a long, frustrating week.

Bruce's initial reaction was to chuckle at what he presumably thought was a joke, but when Emilio kept looking at him seriously and Raul nodded, he seemed to realize Emilio was serious. "Oh," Bruce said in surprise. "Uh, cool."

Emilio tilted his chin toward Bruce in acknowledgement of his comment and then started walking toward the parking lot again.

Bruce trailed along next to him. "So you're sure about that, huh?" he asked.

"Am I sure I'm not romantically attracted to women?" Emilio asked sarcastically and then shook his head. "Yeah, man, I'm sure. Tell your wife she needs to focus on someone else to set up with her sister."

"Yeah, okay," Bruce said with a nod. Then, looking incredibly nervous, he added, "Does that mean you're attracted to me?"

"No way," Emilio answered immediately.

"Oh, okay. Good." Bruce sighed, seemingly relieved to hear this information. But after a matter of seconds, he suddenly glared at Emilio, looking offended. "Why the fuck not?" he asked.

There was no way for Emilio to hold back his laugh. "Calm down, man. It's nothing personal."

Bruce looked down at his body and flexed. His build was similar to Emilio's—thick muscles, broad shoulders, over six feet in height. "Are you saying I'm ugly?" he demanded.

Great. First he got accused of insulting Bruce's wife's appearance, and now it was Bruce directly. Emilio didn't have the energy for this shit. They were getting to the parking lot and his truck was in sight, so he figured the conversation would, mercifully, end soon.

"No, man. I'm just saying you're not my type," he explained.

"What's your type?" Bruce asked disbelievingly.

"Oh, for fuck's sake," Emilio grumbled as he heaved his toolbox into one of the locking equipment boxes in his truck bed. "I cannot believe I'm having this conversation with you. Like I said, it's not personal. I'm into guys who are—" His words were cut short when he looked up and saw the perfect embodiment of his type—the sexy professor was two rows away from them. "Him. He's my type," Emilio said in a rush. "And I'm going to go talk to him. See you Monday." And with those words, he hustled toward the professor, hoping to finally have the chance to hear the intriguing man's voice and wondering if it'd be as mesmerizing as his eyes.

# CHAPTER 2

THOUGH HE had stayed in his office until well after the time the crew working downstairs usually finished for the day, the sound of hammering and sawing and whatever else those tool noises were called had continued. Eventually, Spencer realized the builders were working later than usual. He wanted to go home but didn't want to get caught staring at the hard, sweaty bodies, or, if he was honest, at one particular hot, sweaty body.

For the first few days the construction crew had worked outside of his building, Spencer had enjoyed the eye candy. He'd glance at the men as he walked by and then move on, thinking about his lesson plan or a journal article he was working on. But then one day, he saw a new man working. At least Spencer thought he was new, because he was sure he would have remembered seeing someone handsome enough to grace the cover of a magazine walking around in real life.

The man had been talking with the others, laughing in a carefree way that seemed to take over his whole body. Happiness radiated from him, which was what first caught Spencer's attention. Then he looked over, and for a second,

Spencer lost the ability to breathe. This man was like every naughty fantasy Spencer had ever had come to life, all defined muscles and tanned skin and tight jeans. But none of those fantasies had included warm eyes and soft smiles.

By the time Spencer realized he had been staring and possibly drooling, he knew he had been caught. Fearing an angry reaction from the macho crew, he had dashed away. After that, he had made a point of avoiding them, at least in person. His window gave him a great view of the sexy, joy-filled man.

But now it was Friday, he was tired, and he was trapped in his office. To maintain the up-to-then successful avoidance tactic and yet escape from the building, Spencer decided the best course of action would be to use the rear exit and take the long way to the parking lot. Ten minutes later, with his car in sight, he thought he was free and clear from the tempting man he could never have but couldn't seem to stop wanting. But suddenly he was faced with an unexpected complication: the muscle-bound guy he had been drooling over for weeks was right there, in the parking lot, looking as gorgeous as he had through the window. Spencer hunched down, clutched his leather case to his chest protectively, and hoped he could make it to his car without turning around and staring at the man. Again.

"Hey, hold up!"

Spencer heard the voice behind him and was torn between following the demand or running the remaining few steps to his Accord. Ignoring the person calling out to him would be socially awkward. Not that he was a top authority on social graces, but he was pretty sure running away would be considered rude. So Spencer stopped, took a deep breath, and slowly turned around, keeping his briefcase against his chest.

Of course, he had no idea what kind of protection some leather and paper could offer, or even why he needed protection. Other than the first day he'd seen the handsome man, he hadn't been caught staring. Plus, they were in a public parking lot, in broad daylight. He was safe.

"Hey, uh, hi!" the guy shouted as he jogged over. "I'm Emilio Sanchez."

Now that he was face-to-face with the big man, or actually face to neck, Spencer realized he had been wrong in thinking Emilio was as attractive in person as he had been through the window. No, as it turned out, up close and personal the man was even more stunning. The first time he had walked by the construction site and locked eyes with the stranger, Spencer had turned away within seconds. But this time, the broad chest was right in front of him, the sweat-damp T-shirt stretched over muscles Spencer wanted desperately to touch, and as close as they were standing to each other, the scent of sawdust and musk born of hard work permeated his nose. And that quickly, Spencer felt his cock filling.

Not since he'd been a teenager had he experienced spontaneous erections. And in recent years, he had often found them hard to achieve or maintain even when he was naked in bed with a man. Orgasms, whether alone or with someone, were so infrequent that Spencer couldn't remember the last time he'd had one. He had chalked it up to age, to stress at work, to some bad relationships in his past, to the fact that he hadn't ever had a particularly high sex drive. But none of those factors were stopping him now.

Just a few seconds next to *this* man and Spencer was already achingly hard. Then he gulped and looked up into chocolate-brown eyes and shuddered as his balls drew up and his dick pushed against his zipper. It was as close to coming as he'd been since an unusually active night with his ex over a year prior. Spencer would have been terrified—should have been terrified—that the man in front of him would notice his erection, but it felt so good to want again, to experience that pull in his groin, he couldn't bring himself to feel anything but relief as he lowered his arm so his briefcase covered his bulge.

"We've been doing work close to your office, so I've seen you around," Emilio said, making Spencer realize he had been staring, but not talking. Then the stranger held his hand out and added, "I've wanted to meet you."

"Oh!" Spencer looked down at the offered palm and then back up at the handsome face. He switched his case from his right hand to his left, making sure to keep it in place, shielding his groin. Then he took the man's hand and shook it. "I'm Spencer," he said, proud that his voice shook only a tad. "Spencer Derdinger."

"I was right," Emilio said, sounding quieter, huskier. Spencer waited for clarification about that statement, but it didn't come. Instead Emilio held his gaze and his hand.

"Right about what?" Spencer finally asked, his curiosity getting the better of him.

"That you sound as great as you look."

Not knowing what to say or how to respond, Spencer started blinking rapidly and stammering. "I don't... I... What?"

"What are you doing for dinner tonight?" Emilio asked before Spencer had finished processing the earlier comment.

Feeling completely flummoxed, he didn't know what to say. He looked at his wristwatch instinctively, then back at the man standing in front of him and said, "It's only three thirty."

The contrast between Emilio's shiny white teeth and his deep tan skin and five o'clock shadow made his smile all the more powerful.

"Good point. We shouldn't wait for dinner. Let's start the weekend now."

"Start the weekend... Wait, what are we talking about?" Spencer asked.

"Well, right now we're talking about hanging out for a little while and then getting dinner together." Emilio hadn't moved his gaze from Spencer's face for even a second. He didn't remember ever having someone look at him so intently. It made his legs quake. "But I'm hoping I'll be able to talk you into stretching things out longer. At least until after breakfast."

"Breakfast?" Spencer repeated, hating that he couldn't seem to put together a sentence. He was a numbers guy. Words weren't his specialty and neither were people, so he didn't expect to be charming or a brilliant orator, but a complete sentence would have been nice. Of course, before his mouth could work, his brain would need to catch up to the situation at hand.

"Yes." Emilio raised his free hand and covered the back of Spencer's with it, making him realize they were still holding on from that handshake. "I make a mean omelet," he said as he moved his fingers over Spencer's skin with barely there touches. "Do you have jalapenos?"

"No." Spencer shook his head and then wondered why he had answered the question. The entire conversation made no sense. "But—"

"That's okay. We can always pick some up later. I'll come by now and check your fridge to see what else we'll need."

Truly, the entire conversation was confusing to the point where Spencer wondered if he was dreaming. He half expected a frog to ride by on a flying bicycle at any moment. He could think of only one possible explanation that would lend some logic to the situation, but it seemed very unlikely. No way was this man looking to hook up with him.

At the risk of getting punched, or worse, Spencer steeled his courage and said, "Uh, Emilio." He swallowed hard and took a deep breath. "Are you, uh, coming on to me?"

As soon as he said the words, he realized how ridiculous they sounded. Emilio was all cut muscles, chiseled features, and perfect hair. Someone who looked like that wouldn't have given Spencer a second glance ten years ago, when they would have been closer to the same age. To think it was happening now, when he was softer, grayer, and more lined, was positively preposterous.

But then, contrary to any expectation Spencer had for the response to his question or, for that matter, the entire conversation, Emilio lifted their joined hands to his mouth and gently kissed Spencer's palm. Spencer was pretty sure nobody had done that to him, ever, and it made his heart flutter.

"Yeah, I am," Emilio said. "But if you have to ask, I must not be doing a very good job of it." Emilio grinned as he spoke and his eyes sparkled. "I'll see what I can do to be more clear once we get to your place."

The corners of Spencer's lips tilted up in response. How could he not smile with *this* man looking at him like *that*?

"Oh, holy shit!" Emilio gasped as he let go of Spencer and pressed his own hand against his chest. "You have dimples." He sighed loudly. "I think I'm in love."

Spencer's jaw dropped and all the color drained from his face. "What?"

Without bothering to answer his question, Emilio pointed at Spencer's Honda and asked, "Is this your car?"

Spencer nodded. "I'll follow you to your place, okay?" Emilio didn't wait for an answer, just dipped his face down, planted a kiss on Spencer's cheek, and jogged back to his truck.

It was the single most perplexing exchange of Spencer's life. He wasn't sure what had just happened, what he was supposed to do now, or what was going to happen. With his entire body trembling, he decided to perform simple, familiar tasks: walk, open his car door, put the key in the ignition, and pull out of the parking lot.

He drove home on autopilot, his brain still in that parking lot processing his interaction with the handsome younger man who had looked at him in a completely unfamiliar way. Then he glanced at his rearview mirror and saw the big white truck following him. It was terrifying, like having a freight train barreling straight at him.

No, that was a bad analogy. With a freight train, he'd know what to do—jump out of the way as fast and as far as possible. But this was a gorgeous man with an unexpectedly gentle touch. So, contrary to any logic he should have been smart enough to have or self-preservation instincts he was old enough to have developed, Spencer didn't drive to the nearest police station or a friend's house or a public place. Instead, with his heart slamming against his ribcage, his breath coming out at an unusually fast clip, and his dick still hard as steel, he continued to drive straight home.

EMILIO COULDN'T remember the last time he had been this excited to spend time with a guy. Probably never. He never met men as classy and smart as Dr. Spencer Derdinger at the bars or online, his usual trolling venues.

Though the professor hadn't introduced himself that way, Emilio already knew quite a bit about him after spending two weeks on campus and poking around: Spencer was a math professor, thirty-eight, gay, single, and had published many articles. Emilio had looked them up online and quickly realized he couldn't come close to understanding any of them, which made the man who wrote them all the more impressive. Of course nobody could get a teaching job at a university without being wicked smart, so Emilio wasn't surprised by that information.

From the moment he had laid eyes on the older man, he knew he had to have him. Short brown hair with a hint of gray at his temples, small lines next to his eyes when he squinted as he stepped out of his dark building into the bright sun, and now that adorable blush and dimpled smile. After finally getting the chance to talk to him, Emilio confirmed his suspicions about why the academic had ducked and run the first time they saw each other—Spencer was shy, not pompous. Which meant his personality did it for Emilio as much as his appearance.

It was a heady combination, the sexy maturity mixed with a sweet nervousness. Spencer was this conservative, buttoned-up little package just waiting for Emilio to ruffle it up, tear it open, and see what was hidden from the rest of the world underneath. Emilio groaned and dropped one hand to his lap, pressing the heel of his hand along his erection. He could barely wait to get to the professor's house, where he could slam him up against the wall and fuck him blind.

Minutes later, the silver Honda pulled into the driveway of a cute, if slightly run-down little bungalow. Emilio parked his truck next to the curb and jumped out, ready to pounce on the sexy man he'd been lusting after for weeks. Then he looked, really looked, at Spencer.

The man was standing next to his car, chewing on his bottom lip, holding jingling keys with one trembling hand and his briefcase against his chest with the other. Damn, but did he seem nervous, maybe even scared. Emilio took in a deep breath, slowed his pace, and considered the possibility that maybe this was out of the norm for Spencer.

Did classy guys like this hook up? He figured they must— everyone did—but maybe they didn't do it so fast. Maybe they had wine or something first. He didn't know and didn't have anyone he could text to ask. Well, he'd have to wing it.

Thankfully, unlike his usual hookups, this one was taking place during the light of day and without the brain-fuzzing addition of alcohol, so Emilio had been able to really see Spencer and notice his mood. And now that he was aware of the other man's anxiety, he could change his approach. He still wanted to get off, but he didn't want to scare Spencer away in the process. If that meant going slow, he was game. They could talk first; maybe get into bed instead of screwing up against the door. That'd be okay.

"Great neighborhood," he said, looking around as he spoke. Green yards were scattered with flowering bushes, and the tall trees reached for each other, forming a canopy over the road. "I love all the mature trees. In the newer neighborhoods, every house looks the same and the landscaping is barely grown in." Spencer still looked scared, so Emilio let his instinct guide him. He walked over, gently pried the briefcase from Spencer's clenched fist, and then threaded his fingers with Spencer's, running his thumb over the back of Spencer's smaller hand. "Your house is great. I love Tudors. When was it built? Sometime in the thirties, if I'm guessing right."

After swallowing hard a couple of times, Spencer took in a shaky breath and said, "Yes. It was built in 1934. I bought it a few years ago and planned to fix it up, but I haven't been able to save up enough yet, so right now it's sort of a mix of original and dated remodels."

"That sounds interesting," Emilio said with what he hoped was a soothing smile. "You wanna take me inside and give me the grand tour?"

With another deep inhale and a nod, Spencer started walking toward the steps. "It's not much," he said. "I think of it as the *before* picture. Hopefully someday I'll be able to turn it into the *after*."

"That's okay," Emilio said. He gave Spencer's hand a squeeze and winked when the man looked up at him. "I'm in construction; I'm pretty good at seeing the diamond underneath the rough."

"That's a really beautiful way of looking at things," Spencer replied. He graced Emilio with that soft smile again, the one that made Emilio feel warm inside, and then he unlocked the door and stepped into the house.

Emilio stayed by his side, holding his hand and carrying his briefcase. That small bit of contact was surprisingly nice. It was more tender than the usual groping he engaged in before getting to the main act, keeping his fire stoked without making the flames burn out fast.

"They kept the wood floors," Emilio said, feeling immensely proud of his ability to focus on something other than the man next to him. "They get ripped out and replaced with carpet in so many of these houses, which is a shame. You're lucky to have found one with the floors intact."

"I thought so too," Spencer answered excitedly. "It was one of the features that made me buy it, actually. But now that I've lived here for a while, I've noticed they're in pretty bad shape. There are water rings in some places and gouges in others. I had a flooring company come in to give me a bid on refinishing them last year, but they said it couldn't be done and gave me a quote on new flooring instead."

This was the most animated and least nervous Spencer had been since their first interaction. Apparently, talking about the house made him feel at ease. So Emilio dropped to his knees for a completely different reason than he had anticipated when he had chased the man down.

"Nah, that's bullshit," he said to Spencer after running his hands over the wood. "It'd take a bit of work, but these planks are thick. They were made to be sanded down and refinished, not like today's factory manufactured stuff."

"You think so?" Spencer asked, sounding hopeful. "Even with the water stains and the deep scratches?"

Emilio stayed on his knees and looked up, meeting Spencer's gaze. It was strange being in that position next to a guy he was attracted to, a guy he had come there with the intention of seducing, and not going for his zipper. But Spencer wasn't like other guys; he was someone worth holding on to. And if Emilio wanted a chance at that, he had to treat him better than a quick fuck.

"Yeah," he answered quietly. "If some of the gouges and stains can't be sanded out, they'll add character." Damn, but those eyes were beautiful, the gold strands shining next to the brown. It was hard to keep his hands to himself, so he clenched his fists and forced himself to focus on the conversation. "You'll see. If someone puts hard work into this floor, it'll shine."

# CHAPTER 3

THE SEXIEST man he had ever met or, for that matter, ever seen was in his house, and Spencer was forcing him to talk about refinishing floors. His ex was right; there was something wrong with him.

"I'm sorry," Spencer said. "You didn't come here to work, and I've got you on your hands and knees."

A slow smile crawled up Emilio's face, followed by a light chuckle. "You sure do have a way with words."

Oh God, that had come out all wrong. "I didn't mean... I..."

"It's okay, baby," Emilio said as he slowly raised himself to his feet. "I don't mind giving you a professional opinion on this house."

Being called "baby" stunned him. He was older than Emilio. They'd just met. He wasn't really the endearment type, as proven by the fact that his exes rarely called him anything other than Spencer and maybe the occasional "Spence."

"Should we look at the kitchen next?" Emilio asked.

"The kitchen?"

"Yeah." Emilio took his hand again, like he had outside,

like it was the most natural thing in the world, and started walking through the dining room toward the kitchen. "That's where you want to start the remodeling, right?"

"Yes, but how did you know that? And how do you know where the kitchen is?"

Spencer followed along as he asked the questions. The situation threw him off balance, his head swam, and the only thing stopping him from asking the stranger what was going on was a niggling fear that he already knew. Emilio acted like everything was perfectly normal, and as disconnected as Spencer was to social settings, he had to leave room for the possibility that the only odd thing about the situation was him.

"People usually start with the kitchen when they're remodeling," Emilio said, answering his first question before moving on to the second. "I've been in a lot of these old houses, and they're laid out basically the same way. Entryway leading to a living room on one side and a dining room on the other. The kitchen is behind the dining room, overlooking the backyard, sometimes with a little eating space. The bedrooms and bathroom can be accessed through the living room or a hallway off the kitchen."

The house was small enough that they were standing in the kitchen by the time Emilio finished his explanation. He looked at Spencer and quirked up one corner of his mouth. "How'd I do?" he asked, sounding a little smug. It was sexy. "Did I miss anything?"

Spencer furrowed his brow and said, "I'm not sure how I feel about being so predictable."

With a small tug, he was suddenly pressed against Emilio, chest to chest. The big man cupped his cheek with his free hand and rubbed his thumb under Spencer's chin. "Your house is predictable, not you." He gazed into Spencer's eyes and lowered his voice. "To be honest, this is a little new to me. Hopefully I'm doing all right."

Judging by the erection still throbbing in Spencer's pants, he would have given Emilio high marks. But it wasn't like he could articulate that answer, particularly because he wasn't completely sure what Emilio was asking.

"What's new to you?" he asked. "Do you mean the remodeling work or, uh..." He gulped. "Are you talking about the other, the, uh, coming home with me?"

"Damn, you're cute." Emilio moved his hand through Spencer's hair and massaged his nape. "My family is in construction. There ain't nothin' new about that to me." He grinned again, in that lopsided, self-assured manner. "And I'm pretty good at going home with guys too. But usually that means I get real familiar with their bedrooms." His eyes seemed to darken as he peered at Spencer. "I've never met anyone like you, baby. That's what I meant. So—" He paused. "How am I doin'? Do I got a chance here?"

Either the ground was shaking or he was. This couldn't be real. Things like this didn't happen to Spencer Derdinger: Great-looking men acting like he was some sort of catch.

Hard-ons that wouldn't quit. Free remodeling advice.

"A chance at what?" he asked, needing to understand what he was being asked, needing to know what was going on.

"A chance at you, baby."

"I don't know what that means. How old are you? I'm thirty-eight; that has to be older than you. Why do you keep calling me baby?"

Emilio stepped back and dragged his gaze from Spencer's head to his feet and back again. Then he dipped down and whispered into Spencer's ear. "I'm twenty-two. From the first day I saw you outside of your building, I've wanted you. Being older don't matter. If anything, it's a good thing. I think you're hot as hell. All I need is a chance to show you how it can be between us."

"I have no idea what that means," Spencer whispered.

"It means that you're my baby and I aim to prove it to you. If that word bothers you, I'll use another one," Emilio said. "But it won't change nothing." He leaned back and looked directly at Spencer as he let go of his hand and cupped Spencer's bulge, squeezing and caressing him from balls to dick. "That clear enough?"

Words escaped him at the moment but Spencer gathered the mental power to bob his head in something resembling a nod.

"Good. Now I need to check out your plumbing."

"My plumbing?" Spencer squeaked.

"Yup." Emilio dipped his chin. "Gotta see what shape your pipes are in."

The potential for double entendres was horrifying. "You're talking about my house, right?" Spencer asked.

Emilio threw his head back and laughed. It was as wonderful as when Spencer had heard it that first day, deep and free. "You crack me up," Emilio said. He brushed his lips over Spencer's cheek and then chuckled a little more. "All right. I'm gonna poke around under your sink and then you need to show me your attic access."

"Oh, you don't need to do all of this. Really."

Emilio had the sink open, and he was already on the floor, pulling the few items Spencer kept in there out of the way and then sliding in on his back. "I don't mind. I like working with my hands. Besides, I'm hoping I'll be able to impress you here."

Lying on the floor with his muscular legs spread, Emilio's hard dick was clearly noticeable, stretching across his groin at a slight angle and still reaching his waistband. It looked long and thick, and Spencer instinctively squeezed his rectum in reaction, imagining how it would feel to be stretched by that impressive rod. Then Emilio reached his arms higher and his shirt pulled up, exposing abdominal muscles so defined Spencer would have been sure they were photoshopped had he seen them in a magazine.

Oh. Dear. God.

"I'm impressed," Spencer assured him, his voice sounding

gritty and unfamiliar. "I'm very impressed."

Emilio's husky laugh sounded from beneath the cabinet. "Good to know," he said. "I need to get my tools from my truck." He slid out from under the sink and winked at Spencer. "I can take off my shirt if you want, just wear the tool belt."

Spencer groaned and his breath quickened.

"Yeah?" Emilio sauntered over. "That image doin' it for you, *cariño*?" He cupped Spencer's ass and yanked him forward, putting their groins in direct contact.

"Oh, God." Spencer gasped.

"I do believe this is the most fun I've had on a job." Emilio grinned wickedly. "Ever."

He kissed Spencer again, on the chin this time, and then sauntered out of the kitchen. Spencer was still rooted in place when he heard his front door open and then close. He was panting and throbbing and completely discombobulated. Standing there, waiting for Emilio to come back, he tried to give himself a pep talk.

It was clear that this man wanted to sleep with him, and the feeling was definitely mutual. Usually between the sheets wasn't where Spencer impressed men, but for once, his body seemed to be cooperating. Maybe he should remove his clothes and take Emilio to his bedroom. He was pretty sure things would work out fine, and even if they didn't, he'd get to see Emilio naked. That seemed like reason enough to push ahead with the original purpose for this visit.

But no matter how much his body and mind seemed to

agree on these points, he was still standing in the kitchen when the front door opened again and Emilio called out, "I'm going to take a quick look at the pipes in the bathroom, and then I'll check out the attic." Emilio's boots thumped on the hardwood floors, and Spencer forced himself to move his feet in the direction of the bathroom.

When he walked in, he saw that Emilio hadn't been kidding about the tool belt. He was flat on his back again, the top half of his body under the bathroom sink and the leather tool belt riding low on his hips. Spencer closed his eyes and begged whatever deity might be listening to give him the nerve to move forward with this hookup. Was praying for sex with strangers blasphemous? Spencer decided he didn't care. Getting naked with the sexy man in front of him would be worth whatever repercussions he'd face.

"Okay," Emilio said, his voice sounding closer than it should have.

Spencer's eyes flew open and he found himself looking right at Emilio's neck. Apparently, the man had crawled out from under the sink while he had been praying. He raised his gaze past the dark shadow of Emilio's beard, his full red lips, and his tan skin until he met that dark gaze.

"I think I have a good handle on the pipes," Emilio said. "They're copper, which is great. Unless I see something unexpected in the attic, I don't think you'll need to change those. I seriously doubt you'll be as lucky with the wiring, though. Unless someone replaced it, you'll want to rewire the house and make sure the outlets in the kitchen and bathroom are grounded."

There were any number of appropriate responses to that comment. Spencer could have asked about why pipes made of copper were considered good. He could have asked what it meant to have grounded wires. He could have thanked Emilio for his advice and time.

But instead he said, "You're still wearing a shirt." Then, because that wasn't humiliating enough, he blushed furiously, squeezed his eyes shut again, and started muttering, "Oh, God. Ignore me."

"That's impossible. You are far too cute to ignore." Emilio rubbed his hands up and down Spencer's arms. "I have to keep my shirt on because attics are full of dust and insulation, so we'll need to save the half-naked tool-belt game for another day." At the announcement of the possibility of spending more time with Emilio, Spencer popped his eyes open. That warm gaze was fixed on him, a gentle smile on Emilio's handsome face. "But there is a plus side to this, you know."

Spencer licked his lips, gulped, and said, "What's that?"

"After I'm done up there, I'll be all itchy and grimy, so I'll need to take a shower before we can go to dinner." He paused and then said, "I'm hoping maybe you'll want to join me." He waggled his thick, dark eyebrows. "I promise to take my shirt off before I get in the shower."

As gorgeous as this man was, he was also a little goofy

and gentle and he seemed so genuinely interested that Spencer's nervousness slowly melted away. "Throw in the pants and you've got yourself a deal," he said playfully and held out his hand.

Emilio panned his gaze down to Spencer's hand and then back up to his face. "I ain't shaking your hand," he said.

He cupped Spencer's ass with one hand and tangled his fingers in the back of Spencer's hair with the other. Then he pulled him forward and slammed his mouth against Spencer's in a searing kiss. Emilio kissed like he laughed, like it was a full-body experience. He nibbled and licked at Spencer's lips, sucked on his tongue, massaged his nape and the back of his head, and squeezed his ass. And at the same time, he bent his knees so their groins lined up and then rolled his hips, rubbing their hard dicks together. Spencer was one more grind from coming in his pants when Emilio finally pulled his mouth away, leaving him whimpering and trembling.

"See that?" Emilio said breathlessly. "We sealed it with a kiss. Much better than a handshake."

AS HE climbed up into the attic and away from the handsome man he had just been kissing, Emilio hoped he was making the right move. The moaning, whimpering noises coming from Spencer when they were in the bathroom, combined with the way the man grasped his shoulders and pressed his entire body against Emilio's, were universal signs for "fuck me now." But less than an hour earlier, Spencer had been nervous, maybe even scared, and Emilio wanted to give him more time to adjust to what seemed to be a new experience.

Emilio wondered whether the other man had recently gotten out of a long-term relationship. That would explain why the situation seemed to catch him off guard. Or maybe he wasn't the type to sleep around. It was refreshing, actually.

Emilio's parents had been high school sweethearts and they had recently celebrated their thirty-fifth wedding anniversary. His two oldest brothers had done the same thing, marrying the girls they had dated in high school; his sister, the only one in the family who had attended college, got married right after graduation. Even Henry, who was only three years older than Emilio, was well on his way to getting engaged to a girl he'd been seeing for a couple of years.

Though his current lifestyle of bar pickups and online hookups didn't show it, Emilio wanted the same thing as the rest of his family—someone to build a life with, someone to come home to after a hard day's work, someone to take to Sunday dinners at his parents' house. The guys he met didn't come close to fitting into that picture. They weren't any younger than Emilio, but to him they seemed less settled, like they weren't sure what they wanted to do with their lives other than party a lot and fuck at every opportunity. Not that Emilio had ever complained about either of those things. Hell, he'd always had a good time with the guys he followed home.

But this, here, with Spencer...it felt different, like it was more than a party or a good time for the night, like maybe he had finally met a man who would want the kind of life he pictured in his head. If his instincts were right, Spencer Derdinger could be his forever guy. But Spencer was skittish, reminding Emilio of the feral cats he had found outside his parents' house as a kid. He remembered spending weeks trying to gain their trust—giving them food and letting them get used to his scent—before they'd finally let him touch them and, eventually, bring them into the house.

He hoped like hell it wouldn't take that long to get Spencer into bed, because skittish or not, the man was fucking hot, Emilio had been after him for weeks, and before he had climbed into the attic, Spencer had been looking at him like he wanted to eat him for dinner. Those things were not a combination designed to calm his libido. One way or the other, Emilio was going to have to drain his balls in the shower or he was sure he'd develop a medical condition. He hoped Spencer would want to join him in the task.

IT TOOK close to an hour to follow the trail of tangled wires in the attic, but Emilio wanted to make sure he had a good picture of what Spencer would need to do in order to modernize the house and bring it up to code. Plus, he took the time to develop a plan of how he'd hook his man. Feeling confident that he had the answers on both fronts, Emilio climbed down from the attic.

Before doing anything else, he walked over to the front door and stepped outside. He was standing on the grass, brushing the dust and debris off his clothes, when Spencer shot out the door, looking panicked. He skidded to a halt when he saw Emilio.

"Oh! You're still here," he said.

"You were worried that I took off?" Emilio asked, crooking up one side of his mouth.

"No," Spencer denied unconvincingly. "I heard the door open and—"

"Don't worry," Emilio drawled. "I ain't even gotten started on what I came here to do. I'm not leaving. I needed to get some of this stuff off outside so I wouldn't get your house all dirty."

Spencer relaxed. "Okay," he said, sounding relieved, and then he smiled. "Thank you. That's very considerate."

"I have a change of clothes in my gym bag. It's in my truck," Emilio said, tilting his chin toward the vehicle. "I'll go grab it and then we can take that shower. I'll tell you what I think needs to be done with the house over dinner. That sound okay?"

He figured Spencer would agree, but given the man's shyness to that point, he hadn't expected him to walk off the porch and right into his personal space. But that was exactly what happened.

"Thank you for doing all this," Spencer said when he reached Emilio. He put both hands on Emilio's shoulders, lifted himself up onto the balls of his feet, and placed a soft kiss on the side of Emilio's neck. "I really appreciate it."

Right at that moment, Emilio decided he would do anything Spencer asked, always. Hell, he might try to come up with some stuff Spencer hadn't thought of and do that too. It'd be worth it to get that grateful smile and gentle touch.

He circled his arms around Spencer's waist and rubbed his back. "You're welcome. I hope you'll let me do more, but we can talk about that over dinner too. Right now, I have to get this insulation off me. It's really itchy."

"Oh, okay. Go get your stuff and head for the shower. I'm finishing up some things in the kitchen and then I'll join you." Spencer paused and blushed again. "I mean, if you still want me to."

Just the small contact they'd had outside had made Emilio's dick hard again. He took Spencer's hand and put it over his groin. "Does this answer your question?" he asked huskily.

Spencer shuddered and nodded. "Yes." He swallowed hard. "I'll, uh, just be a minute." He stumbled back into the house on what looked to be shaky legs, making Emilio think he was on the right track.

There was no doubt in Emilio's mind that Spencer was

attracted to him and wanted to go to bed with him. Those things worked strongly in his favor for landing the sweet, intelligent, older man. He figured what he needed to do next was convince Spencer to let him stick around for more than that night. With enough time and enough patience, Emilio was certain he could earn Spencer's trust. And he had the perfect plan to make it happen.

# CHAPTER 4

SPENCER HAD faced some pretty intimidating things in his life. He had defended his dissertation in front of a room full of brilliant scholars. He had come out to parents who he'd accurately predicted wouldn't be accepting. He had moved to a city where he didn't know anybody to start his career. But somehow, not one of those things had been as daunting as getting completely naked in front of Emilio Sanchez.

Even having seen only small portions of the younger man's body, Spencer knew Emilio was built unlike anyone he'd been with, probably unlike anyone he'd seen in real life. And Spencer had sufficient access to a mirror to realize he didn't compare. He didn't consider himself bad-looking, but he knew his looks weren't his best feature. And now he was going to bare everything in a brightly lit bathroom to a man who looked like a fitness model.

It was a terrible idea, sure to result in humiliation and disappointment, but Spencer went through with it anyway. Because the only thing worse than Emilio looking at him in the altogether and changing his mind about wanting to take things further would be spending the rest of his life knowing he'd walked away from a man who was not only incredibly attractive, but also seemed nice and gentle and interested in him. No, Spencer wouldn't walk away. This was a chance worth taking. So he stripped off his clothes, placed them in the laundry basket, and walked into the bathroom.

When he stepped into the shower, Emilio was already under the spray, his head tilted back and eyes closed. That gave Spencer a chance to assess the complete picture of the man who had inexplicably followed him home. The mere fact that he didn't swallow his tongue in reaction to the sight before him warranted a prize.

Whatever image Spencer previously had of physical perfection was dwarfed by the specimen of male beauty before him: cut muscles on his stomach and hips, no discernible body fat, thickly veined arms, large, low-hanging balls, and a dick that looked only half-hard but still more than long and thick enough to stretch him in the best way possible. He moaned at the sight, clueing Emilio in to his presence.

The beautiful man stepped out of the shower stream, wiped his palms over his eyes, and then blinked them open, landing his sparkling gaze right on Spencer. It wasn't a particularly large space, so there wasn't a lot of room to spare, but it didn't matter, because Emilio immediately wrapped his arms around Spencer's nude body and drew him close. "Hey," he said with a smile. "Fancy meeting you here."

"Wow," Spencer said as he ran his hands across Emilio's shoulders and down his flanks. "You have an amazing body."

Emilio bent forward and kissed his way across Spencer's jaw as he maneuvered him toward the wall and pressed him up against it. "I'm glad you think so." He put his hands on either side of Spencer's neck and dipped his face down, whispering, "I like the way you look too, *cariño*," right before he moved his lips over Spencer's in a passionate kiss.

With a soft touch, Emilio ran his fingers over Spencer's neck and licked and sucked at his lips. Spencer moaned and opened for him, kissing him back as he rubbed his hands over all the slick muscles in Emilio's back and round, firm ass.

"Mmm," Emilio moaned. "Feels good." He rolled his hips so their dicks settled side by side, and then ground himself against Spencer as he continued his devouring kiss and his constant touches.

As he had when Emilio kissed him earlier, and, for that matter, when Emilio had done nothing more than speak to him, Spencer hardened in reaction to this man's attention. It felt amazing, so he moved against the hard body, rubbing and touching and kissing. Then, completely uninvited, the memories of his previous sexual encounters entered his mind.

Yes, he had an erection right now, which was a wonderful improvement, but what if he couldn't maintain it? What if he couldn't come? What would Emilio say or think? Peter, Spencer's ex, had been several years older than him, and while sex between them had been frustrating for Spencer, on the rare occasions they'd had it, Peter seemed satisfied so long as he got off.

"Hey." Emilio moved his hand from Spencer's head, down his cheek, and over to the side of his neck. "What happened?" he asked as he rubbed his thumb over Spencer's skin. "Where'd you go?"

Too ashamed to face Emilio's gaze, Spencer looked down and said, "I'm right here. I don't know what you mean."

Not stopping the soothing back-and-forth movement of his right thumb, Emilio held on to Spencer's shoulder with his left hand and maintained the pressure of his pelvis against Spencer's, keeping him in place.

"Listen, Spencer, I know we just met, but I'm a jump-in kind of guy. When I see something I want, I tend to go after it, and I've been wanting you forever. But I'm not looking to push you or anything. If you need me to slow my ass down, tell me. Just because I won't like it don't mean I won't listen, all right?" He moved his thumb under Spencer's chin and tipped it up until their gazes met. "My mama's always sayin' I gotta learn how to be patient. But I've been waiting since the first day I saw you, so to me, this thing has been a long time coming." He shrugged and looked sheepish as he said, "I get that you might not feel the same way, and I'm sorry if I'm movin' too fast here."

For as short as it was, Emilio's speech managed to evoke several emotions in Spencer. He was undeniably attracted to Emilio's take-charge attitude and yet comforted by his sensitivity and willingness to move at what he perceived to be

Spencer's pace. He was impressed by the maturity displayed by someone so young and charmed by the hallmarks of that very youth sprinkled in—like considering a couple of weeks to be *forever*.

But the most prominent feeling within Spencer was a need to ease Emilio's worry. He didn't want the other man to think he'd done anything wrong or to believe that his desires weren't returned, because neither of those things was true. So even though it was awkward and more than a little bit embarrassing, he decided to be honest.

"It's not that." He swallowed hard. "I do want you, Emilio. So much. But you should know that I'm not really, uh..." Saying the words was difficult enough, but choosing them seemed to be even harder. "I've never really been good at this," he finally admitted. "I don't always—" He looked down at his semi-hard dick and then back up at Emilio. "It might not stay...you know...and you're so..." He dragged his gaze over Emilio's handsome face and ripped chest and felt a sharp need low in his belly, making him shudder. "God, you're so gorgeous, and you've been so nice. I don't want to disappoint you."

"For real?" Emilio asked, sounding joyful. "That's what's got you worried?" It was an unexpected reaction, to be sure, but Spencer managed to nod. Emilio chuckled and pulled Spencer in for another kiss. "You don't gotta worry about that, *cariño*. I may not understand most of the things you write or teach, but this—" He dropped his hand between their bodies and rolled Spencer's balls. "I got this covered."

Having a conversation about erectile dysfunction wasn't ever on Spencer's wish list, and talking about it when his dick was, at that very moment, filling and throbbing, was too much. He had said his piece, had warned Emilio. Now he wanted to stop worrying and thinking. He wanted to revel in the feelings those large hands, hard body, and soft lips were infusing in him.

"Let's get you washed. We'll add one of those fancy glass showers and a bigger water heater to the remodeling list. But for now, we need to get out of the shower before we freeze our nuts off and I won't be able to show you how loud I can make you scream when you drain them."

"Jesus." Spencer panted in reaction to the rough, dirty words.

People he knew didn't talk that way, and he wouldn't have thought he'd find it arousing, but like everything else about Emilio, it made him want even more. He made quick work of washing his hair and reached for the shower gel and sponge, but Emilio beat him to it.

"Can I wash you?" he asked. "I'd really like that." When Spencer dropped his arms and bobbed his head, Emilio smiled broadly. "Thank you."

He lathered the sponge and moved it over Spencer's shoulders and chest, washed under his arms and down his sides. Then he squatted and lathered Spencer's legs, lifted each foot so he could soap it up, and reached for Spencer's blessedly hard dick, stroking it as he cleaned.

"Ah!" Spencer threw his head back and cried out when Emilio cupped his balls with his other hand, manipulating both organs in tandem.

Just when Spencer thought he might come, Emilio stopped rubbing and steered him under the shower spray, rinsing all the lather off his body.

"Turn around, *cariño*," Emilio said, his voice sounding low and husky. He raised himself back up to a standing position. "I need to get your back now."

With every muscle trembling and his skin feeling hypersensitive, Spencer slowly turned around and flattened his hands against the tile. It was fine at first, but then he could feel a body behind him, hear someone moving, and though his brain knew it was Emilio, he couldn't see.

"I don't... I can't..." He flipped around so he was facing Emilio again and immediately relaxed when he could confirm with all his senses that Emilio was the man touching him.

Confusion flitted over Emilio's face, followed by anger, making Spencer cringe.

"I'm sorry," Spencer said. "I want you to touch me, it's—"

Emilio circled those huge hands around him and pulled him close once again. "Don't apologize," he said. "I'll fucking kill him if I find out who he is, but don't you apologize."

Before he could process how quickly Emilio had understood the reason for his reluctance, the man rubbed his still soapy hands over Spencer's back and ass, then dipped his fingers into Spencer's crease, touching, caressing, and effectively distracting him from anything and anyone who came before.

"This feel okay?" Emilio whispered. When Spencer whimpered and nodded, he moved his hand over Spencer's crack and edged two fingers inside, slid them over the clenching pucker, and rubbed it in slow circular movements with lightly increasing pressure. And all the while, he petted Spencer's hair, nibbled on his jaw, neck, and ear, and rocked their pelvises together. "Can I go in, *cariño*?" he asked, and Spencer strongly suspected the question was for him alone, that Emilio wouldn't be so hesitant with other men. "Just my finger today," Emilio promised when he didn't immediately respond.

"Yes," Spencer said quietly. "I'm sorry you have to—"

Emilio moved his lips over Spencer's, silencing his apology. He kissed and licked his way into his mouth at the same time he pushed a thick finger into Spencer's hole.

"Oh!" Spencer grabbed onto Emilio's shoulders and went up on tiptoe. "It's good," he said, looking right into Emilio's eyes.

"I know," Emilio said, a world of understanding in his expression. "I promise to make sure you always feel good when you're with me." He crooked his finger and found Spencer's gland, tapping it lightly and making Spencer's body sing.

"Uh," Spencer groaned as his eyes rolled back. He leaned

forward, letting Emilio support him. "I love this. I'd forgotten how much I love this."

"I'll remind you," Emilio said as he tapped deep inside a few more times. Then he slowly removed his finger and rinsed the soap off Spencer. "The water's cold. Time to get out." He turned off the tap and helped Spencer dry off and get out of the shower.

THERE ARE certain experiences that haunt you forever. For Emilio, at the top of that list was a night when he was eight years old and his then eighteen-year-old sister Alicia came home from a date. Raul, his oldest brother, had moved out by then. Emilio had been asleep in bed in the room he shared with his brother, Henry, when loud voices woke them. They snuck out into the hall and tried to hear what was going on without being seen.

Though he didn't have a clear memory of everything he heard and saw, Emilio remembered Alicia crying, his brother Martin storming out of the house, his mother taking his sister to the hospital, and then, once everyone was gone, his father sitting on the couch and shaking as tears streamed down his face. It was probably the last part that made the night stick in his mind because Emilio had never seen his big, strong father cry.

Many years later, when he was in high school and his family mistakenly thought he was dating girls, his sister asked him to come to her house to help with something. When he arrived, Alicia's husband and baby son were gone and she was sitting at her kitchen table with a plate of cookies and a couple of sodas. His parents had never had the birds and the bees talks with their kids, but growing up with three older brothers meant Emilio had a good handle on the mechanics, so he was surprised when Alicia said she wanted to talk to him about sex. But twenty minutes later, when he hugged his teary-eyed sister and left her house, he remembered that night from before, remembered what he'd seen and heard when he was eight. And then he understood what Alicia meant about always, always knowing that he was stronger than girls and that unless they said yes, actually *said* it, he had to assume they meant no.

Already knowing he was gay, Emilio had brushed the lesson aside as something that would never impact him. But when Spencer had tensed in the shower, the look of abject fear on his face as he'd turned around, Emilio realized he'd been wrong. He recognized that fear, that humiliation, because he'd seen it on Alicia's face that night long ago, had even seen traces of it that day at her kitchen table. Suddenly he was grateful for that talk with his sister, for the lesson she had taught him, because gay or straight turned out not to be the issue at all. And now he knew to be extra careful with his smart little professor until he earned his trust.

"Tell me what you like," he whispered into Spencer's ear as he steered them toward the bedroom. He kept both hands on the smaller man, touching and caressing every part of his body. "Do you like being touched?" He fisted Spencer's dick and gave it a few strokes. "Do you like being sucked?" He drew Spencer's earlobe into his mouth and worked it with his tongue as he suckled it. "Do you like to bottom or top?" He squeezed Spencer's firm globes and moved his fingers into his channel, petting the sensitive skin.

Seemingly unable to answer with words, Spencer moaned and whimpered in response to every question and touch. By the time they reached the bedroom, Spencer was flushed and panting. Emilio backed himself up to the bed. He kissed Spencer gently and stroked his cheek before sitting on the mattress. Then, with his gaze locked with Spencer's, he scooched until he was in the middle of the mattress.

"C'mere, *cariño*," he said as he reached his hand out to Spencer. The other man didn't hesitate before crawling right across the mattress and onto Emilio's lap. He straddled Emilio's bigger body, placed a knee against each side of Emilio's waist and dragged his erection across Emilio's stomach. "Mmm, that's it," Emilio mumbled as he planted one hand on the mattress to brace himself and tangled the other in Spencer's hair, pulling his face down. "You feel so good on me," he whispered right before tugging Spencer's lower lip between his and flicking his tongue over it.

"Oh," Spencer moaned. He circled his arms around

Emilio's neck, combed his fingers through Emilio's hair, and then started rocking up and down, giving both of their hard dicks much needed friction. "Is this okay?" he asked, his voice sounding husky.

"Yeah, feels perfect." Emilio leaned back so he could meet Spencer's gaze and said, "You take what you need, okay? As long as you're with me in this bed, I'm going to be into whatever we do. Hell, I'm pretty sure I can get off just by looking at you and listening to you read some of those papers I don't understand."

Spencer clutched Emilio's hair and kissed him desperately. "How are you real?" he whispered before going back for more, sliding his lips against Emilio's and then sucking on his tongue while he continued rolling his hips.

In their current position, Emilio's dick was trapped between their bodies, pressed against his stomach. But as they continued kissing, Spencer rocked higher and higher, sometimes causing Emilio's cock to nudge Spencer's balls. After it happened a couple of times, Spencer pulled away from Emilio's mouth and got onto his knees. He looked down at Emilio's swollen, red-tipped dick and moaned as he pulled it down and then sat over it, wedging it against his balls and between the cheeks of his firm ass. Then he started rocking again, and Emilio felt like he had died and gone to heaven.

"Oh, shit," he said. "Like that. Just like that." He yanked Spencer down and sucked his tongue into his mouth, tangling it with his own as he raised his hips up to meet Spencer's downward motions.

It didn't take long after that, not with the way they were feeding from each other, touching each other's faces, pulling each other's hair, and rolling their bodies in tandem, giving each other much needed pressure.

Just as Emilio was about to lose it, Spencer yanked his mouth back and stared at him. His eyes were wide, shocked, his mouth open in a large O, and he didn't stop the movement of his hips for even a second. "I'm gonna," he said. "I can't believe...I..." He looked down between their bodies, seemingly surprised by the sight of his own erect dick. "It's been so long, but I think...I..."

Emilio flattened his palm on Spencer's lower back and held him close as he ratcheted up the speed and power of his thrusts from below. "Fuck, yeah, Spencer, take what you need. Show me how good it is. Let me feel you cream. Wanna smell it on me all night."

Whether it was his words or his motions, Emilio didn't know, but Spencer bucked hard, cried out his name, and then shouted as his dick exploded, pulsing endless streams of ejaculate across Emilio's stomach and chest. Between the sights and sounds of Spencer finding his pleasure and the feeling of Spencer's ass and balls rubbing against his dick, Emilio was right there with him, calling out Spencer's name as he came.

They were both still breathing hard when they brought their lips together again, the kisses more gentle this time, slowing with the pace of Spencer's thrusts until he melted against Emilio, rested his cheek on Emilio's shoulder, and hugged him tightly. Emilio rubbed circles on Spencer's back and felt him shudder and push even closer.

"Good?" Emilio asked as he turned his face and kissed Spencer's forehead. His man nodded and whimpered, holding on for dear life. "Good." Emilio sighed as he lowered his back to the bed until he was lying down with Spencer's smaller frame blanketing him. "Good."

# CHAPTER 5

HE HAD come. Not alone after working himself for so long motion burns were sure to appear the next day. And not after taking medications that made his heart race or his head hurt. No, he had come while he was with a man after doing nothing other than kissing and rubbing for a matter of minutes. Happiness bubbled up from Spencer's chest, and he started laughing, the joy overwhelming.

"What're you laughing at?" Emilio asked. He gave Spencer's ass a little squeeze. "You're gonna give me a complex or something."

Spencer flattened his palms against the mattress on either side of Emilio's broad shoulders and then straightened his arms and gazed into Emilio's shining eyes. "I'm just really happy," he admitted, even though he realized it might sound a little weird.

"Oh yeah?" Emilio asked, looking very pleased with himself. He stretched his neck a tad and bumped his nose against Spencer's before giving him a soft kiss. "I did okay, huh?" He chuckled. "Does that mean I earned an invite to stay for a repeat performance? Or do I need to rewire a lamp or something first?"

"You can rewire lamps?" Spencer asked, trying to sound serious but unable to keep the huge grin off his face for more than a second.

Emilio threw his head back and laughed deeply. God, but did Spencer love that laugh.

"Goofball," Emilio said and then goosed him.

"Hey!" Spencer leaped a little, moving away from the unexpected pinch on his ass. "Be nice!"

"Want me to kiss it and make it better?" Emilio asked, and then he crooked one side of his lips up and waggled his eyebrows. Spencer's breath hitched and he made a noise that sounded like a mix between a gasp and a hiccup. "Oh yeah," Emilio said smugly. "I think we already know one thing to add to tonight's agenda. If you'll answer my questions from before, we can make it a complete list."

"Your questions?"

"Yup." Emilio held on to Spencer and rolled them onto their sides, keeping them connected from chest to feet. "I wanna know what you're into, what you like in bed."

"Oh." Spencer blushed. "Just the same stuff as everyone else, I guess. I liked what we just did. I like when you touch me." He reached his hand up to Emilio's mouth and traced his lips with a finger. "I like your mouth."

"Is that code for you like getting sucked off?"

How Emilio could say the words so casually, Spencer didn't know, but he was going to have to get his blush reflex under control around this man. "Who doesn't?" he asked.

Emilio snorted and said, "Good point."

The conversation wasn't nearly as uncomfortable as it should have been. In fact, Spencer was having a good time. It motivated him to continue talking.

"And as far as the other," he said, "I like to bottom. I mean, I can top if I need to, but…" He looked at Emilio from underneath his lashes. "I don't know. I like bottoming better, I guess, as long as it's not in certain positions. From behind's my favorite position." He shrugged and whispered, "Or at least it used to be. It's been a while."

Emilio combed his fingers through Spencer's hair gently. "You'll tell me what the bad positions are, right? Because to me, any position that involves my dick in your ass is gonna be a good one. I can tell you that right now."

"Very funny," Spencer said with a smile and a little shake of his head.

"I ain't kidding," Emilio responded. "You have a nice butt. I wanna do a lot of wicked things to it."

He heard himself make another of those new hiccup-moan noises and knew if they didn't get out of bed soon, he'd be asking Emilio to get started on the wicked things right away. It wasn't a bad idea, actually, but Emilio had to be hungry after doing physically grueling work all day and then working more when he got to Spencer's house.

"I made dinner," Spencer said. "I know you talked about going out to eat, but I'm a decent cook and I had time while you were in the attic, and it was really nice of you to help me, so..." He shrugged. "But if you want to go out, that's fine too."

"You made me dinner?" Emilio asked, his face lighting right up. "You're so sweet." He cupped Spencer's cheek and kissed the tip of his nose.

Spencer beamed. "It's nothing fancy," he explained. "Just chicken with a mushroom sauce, baked kale, and a salad."

Right on cue, Emilio's stomach growled. "Damn," he groaned. "Cute as hell, super smart, great in bed, and you cook too?" He shook his head. "I ain't ever letting you go."

The statement sent a pang of need and hope right through Spencer's chest. He forced himself to stay calm and remember that Emilio seemed to use words in a more free and less literal way than other people. That comment was the man's way of thanking him for making dinner, not an actual expression of a desire to date Spencer forever or even long-term. Spencer was old enough to know that a man didn't go home with someone he just met for anything more than a round or two of sex, and he wasn't naïve enough to think sex—even good sex—would keep that man coming back for more. He mentally repeated those reminders three times so he wouldn't be disappointed when later that night or, if he was lucky, the next day, Emilio did what any normal person would do—go home and keep living his life in exactly the same way as he had before they'd met.

Spencer leaned forward, pressed his lips to the hollow of Emilio's throat, and inhaled deeply. He wanted to keep that moment in his memory for later, when he was alone again. Emilio's grip on him tightened, and Spencer felt moisture in his eyes. A couple of calming breaths got his emotions under control.

"Ready to eat?" he asked.

"Oh yeah." Emilio's stomach growled again. He arched his eyebrows. "See?"

With a snort and a smile, Spencer rolled off the bed. "Okay. Everything's ready, so we'll be able to tame that beast inside your belly fast." He slipped into his white briefs and a long-sleeve shirt, then pulled a pair of jeans out of his closet and turned to face Emilio as he started putting them on. "If you have a sweet tooth, I can—"

Oh. Dear. God.

Emilio was still nude, and he was bent over, shuffling through his duffel bag, giving Spencer a front-row view of the most gorgeous ass on the planet along with those huge balls and the pretty cock.

Spencer must have made a noise of some sort because, suddenly, Emilio twisted his upper body and said, "Are you okay?" He sounded worried.

"I'm... Yes... Fine."

That slow, sexy grin made another appearance, and Emilio's eyes twinkled. He stood, sauntered over, and curled his hands around Spencer's clenched fists. Spencer relaxed his hold on his jeans, letting them drop to the floor, and twined his fingers with Emilio's.

"Were you checking out my ass?" Emilio asked in a husky whisper.

Though he opened his mouth to answer with words, a strangled whine came out instead.

"Fuck," Emilio groaned. "You look at me like that and I want to take you back to bed." He moved one hand up Spencer's arm, causing Spencer to tremble and lean closer to him. "Ever since I saw you at the university that first time, all buttoned up and shy, I couldn't stop wondering what you'd be like when I got you alone." He squeezed Spencer's shoulder and then dragged that big hand up Spencer's neck to his cheek. Reflexively, Spencer turned into Emilio's palm and nuzzled it. "You're even better than I imagined. So sensual and sweet, on top of being crazy smart." He shook his head in apparent disbelief. "How did I get this lucky?"

Spencer had been asking himself the very same question.

Emilio bent down and licked his earlobe. "Tell me you don't have plans this weekend," he said, his voice low. "Tell me we can spend the next two days trying to figure out how many times we can get off before we pass out."

"Jesus," Spencer gasped.

"Say I can stay, *cariño*."

Needing a moment to make the world stop spinning and gather his wits, Spencer changed the topic and said, "You keep calling me that." He swallowed hard. "It's Spanish, right? What does it mean?"

"*Cariño*?" Warm, soft lips kissed the side of his neck,

making him tremble.

"Uh-huh."

"It means darling." Emilio kissed his way down the side of Spencer's neck. "Honey." He licked a long swathe up over his Adam's apple. "Sweetheart." He tugged Spencer's lower lip between both of his. "Love." Then he pulled back and pierced Spencer with his deep, dark gaze. "Say I can stay, *cariño.*"

With his heart slamming against his ribs and his voice so scratchy it wasn't recognizable, Spencer said, "You can stay."

Emilio tangled one hand in the back of Spencer's hair, tipped his head back, and gripped his hip with the other, then yanked him forward. Spencer knew what was coming and he welcomed it. He clutched Emilio's arms right above his elbows, closed his eyes, and parted his lips. When the kiss came, it was softer than Spencer had expected, a gentle exploration of mouth and tongue. He didn't know how long they stayed that way, holding on to one another, but eventually Emilio's stomach rumbled again and they broke apart.

"You finish getting dressed. I'll get the food on the table," Spencer said.

"Okay." Emilio gazed at him for another moment before going back to his duffel bag.

Spencer bent down to retrieve his discarded jeans, made quick work of putting them on, and walked out of the room, intent on finding out whether there was even a kernel of truth in the old adage that the way to a man's heart was through his stomach.

EMILIO WATCHED Spencer walk out of the room, listened to his footsteps retreating down the hall, and then snatched his cell phone from the bundle of clothes he'd stripped off before the shower. He sat on the edge of the bed and dialed.

His brother Henry answered after a couple of rings. "Yo. What up?"

"Hey. I got a question for you," Emilio said. "Why haven't you married Stacy yet?"

There was a pause and then Henry snapped at him, "What the fuck, man? I don't hear enough of this shit from her friends, now I gotta hear it from you too?"

Ignoring the outburst, Emilio pressed forward. "Seriously. You've been together how long? Two years, right? You should have babies and shit by now. What's holding you up?"

Another pause. "Two and a half. And what's with the sudden interest in my relationship? You never gave a shit about my personal life before."

"That's not true," Emilio said. "I care."

"About me?" Henry asked. "Yeah. About what I have going on with Stacy or any other girlfriend? No."

"Well, I'm asking now. Two and a half years is a long time. Don't you want to lock it up? Get married, move in together, have kids? Don't you want what Ma and Pop have?"

The pause was much longer this time, and Emilio could hear Henry pacing. "That's just it, bro," he eventually said. "It isn't like that with her. That's why I haven't wanted to get married. But she's great, so I keep thinking maybe I need more time and then it'll be different. Maybe the way Ma and Pop are is because they've been together a long time, you know? Maybe it ain't something that happens right away, and you gotta grow into it."

Emilio rolled the idea over in his mind. "You really think it works that way?" he finally asked.

Henry sighed loudly. "I don't know," he said, sounding sad. "I really don't. You gonna tell me what's up with all the questions?"

"I met someone," Emilio confessed.

"Yeah? That guy you been scoping out at the UNLV job?"

"How'd you know about that?" Emilio asked in surprise.

"Raul told me. He ain't stupid. You think he doesn't know why you been hanging around that job site so much?"

Emilio chuckled. His family was a little overbearing. Okay, a lot overbearing. But he was lucky to have them. Henry was his best friend, followed by his other two brothers, and there wasn't a more caring person on earth than his sister.

"Yeah. That's the guy," he confirmed. "His name's Spencer."

"So? What's he like? Some brainy college boy?"

"Brainy college *professor*. And he's not just smart. He's..."
Emilio tried to find the right words to describe the cute, kind
man at the other end of the house. "He has this smile that's,
like, shy but sexy at the same time. The first time I saw it, it
was like a punch to the gut, man. I'm telling you." He shook his
head at the memory and rubbed his stomach, remembering
how he'd felt that first day. "And he's really successful. He
has a job at UNLV and owns his house, but there's something
about him that makes me feel like he needs me, like maybe
even though he's older and shit, I can take care of him and
he'd let me. And he made me this great dinner. I mean, I
haven't tasted it yet, but it sounds like it's gonna be really
good. And he dresses all conservative, but when the clothes
come off, he's—"

"It doesn't take time to grow into it, does it?" Henry
asked sadly.

"I don't think so," Emilio responded, understanding
exactly what Henry meant. "Sorry."

His brother sighed deeply. "He sounds great. When're
you gonna bring him around?"

"I don't know yet. Hopefully soon. I'm still working on
getting him used to me. I don't wanna scare him off with the
force of the whole Sanchez clan at once."

"'Kay. Well, if you wanna start in small doses, let me
know," Henry said. "We can go grab a beer and shoot some
pool."

"Will do," Emilio responded. "Thanks."

"I'm happy for you, bro. Talk to you later."

With a feeling of warmth in his chest and a smile on his face, Emilio dropped the phone into the side pocket of his gym bag and started pulling his clothes out. After a moment of hesitation, he left everything other than his workout shorts in the bag. He stepped into the shorts and pulled them up to just above his hips.

There was no way to miss the fact that Spencer liked looking at Emilio's body. Plus, the man had admitted it. Hopefully walking out dressed in nothing but the loose, thin shorts would keep Spencer interested and on edge, so he'd be receptive to Emilio's plan. After a pit stop in the bathroom to clean up, Emilio checked himself out in the mirror. He shoved his hand down the front of his shorts and gave his dick a couple of tugs, wanting it to fill a bit, then he strutted out of the room and over to the kitchen.

Maybe it was because Emilio was barefoot. Or maybe it was because Spencer was distracted. But most likely it was because Spencer was so clearly nervous. Whatever the reason, he didn't hear Emilio approach. When he reached the dining room doorway and saw Spencer, Emilio froze mid-swagger.

The small, round table was crowded with fabric place mats, brightly colored plates holding perfectly arranged food, water glasses, a water pitcher, wine glasses, a bottle of wine, a bread basket, and candlesticks. Spencer stood next to the table. He moved one of the plates an inch to the right, switched the placement of the bread and wine bottle before putting them back where they had been to begin with, and then hovered over the candles, lighter in hand.

He furrowed his brow and chewed on his bottom lip, seemingly putting great thought into something. Eventually, he picked the candles up, walked into the kitchen with them, put them in a drawer, and closed it. Then he stared at the drawer, still in deep thought, opened it again, picked the candles up, and walked to the table, only to turn back around, candles still in hand.

It was obvious Spencer was trying hard to put together a nice meal. And that he was more than a little anxious about it. Emilio's heart melted and his game plan changed. This man wanted him already; seduction wasn't necessary. But if he wanted to stay around long enough to see whether their mutual attraction could turn into something lasting, Emilio would need to make Spencer feel comfortable and safe. Because if he continued at his current level of anxiety, he'd either make himself sick or toss Emilio out to preserve his own sanity.

"Hey, *cariño*," Emilio said, making sure to keep his voice low so he wouldn't startle the distracted, nervous man in front of him.

Spencer jerked his head toward the doorway and looked at Emilio then down at the candles in his hands before looking at Emilio again, a blush creeping up his neck like he had been caught with his hand in the cookie jar.

"It looks real nice in here," Emilio said as he slowly approached Spencer. He bent down, kissed Spencer's cheek, and then gently took the candles from his hands. "You know, nobody's ever done anything like this for me before," he confessed. "We only ever have tablecloths and candles on Christmas at my *abuelita's* house." He placed the candles on the table, where they'd been before Spencer moved them, and then looked up and met Spencer's gaze. "Makes me feel real good that you went to all this trouble. Thank you."

When the tension eased from Spencer's body, Emilio instantly felt better.

"It wasn't any trouble," Spencer assured him as he walked over. "What about..." He paused and bit his bottom lip. Emilio could tell from Spencer's expression that he was trying to decide whether he should finish his question.

If their too-short time in the bedroom had been any indication, Spencer seemed to be more at ease when they were touching. That seemed like as good an excuse as any to do what he wanted anyway—hold Spencer tight—so Emilio opened his arms. Even the orgasm he'd just had didn't beat the feeling of satisfaction that coursed through him when Spencer walked over without hesitation, circled his arms around Emilio's waist, and rested his face against Emilio's broad chest. Emilio wrapped his strong arms around Spencer's shoulders and held him close.

After a few moments, Spencer quietly asked, "What

about your boyfriends? I bet they made you nice dinners all the time."

"Nope." Emilio shook his head and combed his fingers through Spencer's soft hair.

"No?" Spencer sounded scandalized. He looked up at Emilio, his eyes wide with surprise. "How is that possible? You're amazing. If I was your boyfriend, I'd be falling all over myself trying to..."

It looked like Spencer's words caught up with his brain at that exact moment, because he stopped talking midsentence, turned an almost crimson color, and buried his face in Emilio's neck.

"I guess I ain't met the right kind of guys." Emilio ran his hand down the back of Spencer's head and, when Spencer looked up, kissed his forehead and mumbled, "Until now."

# CHAPTER 6

BEING WITH Emilio was a completely foreign experience for Spencer; it was nothing like the few one-night stands he'd had, or the start to any of his previous relationships. Meeting new people was difficult for him, so once he got to know someone, he tried to hang on. Plus, he enjoyed being part of a couple—having someone to call when something good happened at work, someone to sit with at the movies, someone by his side when an occasion called for a plus one. That had resulted in a series of semi-long-term relationships, so Spencer didn't consider himself a novice when it came to commitment.

But usually the commitment came after a period of time dating and getting to know a guy. After that point, there was generally a careful dance about how often to call, how much time to spend together, and how to articulate feelings without pushing too hard or clinging too much. The bottom line was that Spencer was accustomed to spending time warming up on the deck, then dipping his toes in the water, and maybe eventually hanging around in the shallow end while he tried to decide whether it was safe to tread where the water level hit higher than his waist. So far, the farthest he'd gone was mid-chest.

He blinked at the gorgeous man gazing down at him and found himself more than a little out of breath. Being with Emilio was like diving headfirst into the deep end of the pool. Emilio petted and caressed him with a big, warm hand, eventually landing on his chest.

"Your heart is racing. What're you thinking about so hard?"

"Swimming," he answered.

"Swimming?" Emilio repeated, looking surprised by that answer.

Spencer nodded.

"Huh. What about it?" Emilio asked.

"Well." Spencer licked his lips. "It can be dangerous, you know. I mean, even if you have experience in the, uh, pool. You can swim out to the middle, thinking everything's fine, and then, out of nowhere, you get a leg cramp or something. It happens. And you're too far from the wall, so the next thing you know, you're going under."

"I see." Emilio nodded slowly. "Well, I think there's only one way to make sure that doesn't happen."

Spencer thought the same thing, but he wasn't ready to say it yet. He thought they could share a meal and spend the night together first. Maybe even the weekend.

"The way I see it," Emilio said while he rubbed circles on Spencer's chest with one hand and caressed his nape with the other, "the way to make sure you don't drown is to never go swimming alone. If you're with someone brave enough to jump in with you and strong enough to hold you above the water until the cramp passes, then you'll be safe."

They weren't talking about swimming. At least *he* wasn't talking about swimming, and he was pretty sure Emilio was on the same page.

"But how do you know if you can rely on your, uh, swim partner to take care of you like that?" Spencer asked. "How can you be sure he'll keep you safe?"

"That's the toughest part," Emilio agreed. "You gotta find someone you trust. That can be pretty hard, especially if you've been let down before."

"How do you do that?" Spencer asked, his voice barely louder than a whisper. "How do you know who you can trust?"

"Well..." Emilio paused and seemed to be giving the question serious thought. He moved his hand down to Spencer's belly. "I'd listen to my gut." He dragged his palm up to Spencer's chest. "I'd listen to my heart." He leaned down and kissed Spencer's cheek before whispering in his ear, "That's how I'd decide if the guy is good enough to take swimming."

"I don't... My gut isn't always..." Spencer swallowed hard, unsure how to articulate what he felt.

"Shh, it's okay, *cariño*." Emilio brushed his fingers through Spencer's hair. "I got a new idea. My gut tells me I can trust you at the pool. So, for now, how about you be my swim partner, make sure I don't get hurt? And in return, I'll keep an eye on you too. Maybe eventually, your gut'll tell you it's okay to go for a swim." He smiled down at Spencer, his eyes warm and understanding. "How's that sound?"

"That's not... It's not fair, is it? To you, I mean. It doesn't sound fair."

"Nah, don't you worry about that." Emilio waved his hand, seeming completely unconcerned about equity. "I don't mind playing lifeguard. It's all good."

Spencer took a long, fortifying breath and gave Emilio a shaky smile. "I've never met anybody like you."

"I hope that's a good thing." Emilio gave him one of his lopsided grins.

"It is." Spencer bobbed his head. "It's a very good thing." *A very, very good thing.*

"Cool." He kissed Spencer's forehead. "So now you gonna feed me or what? 'Cause I'm ready to refuel and whatever you made smells great."

"Oh!" Spencer's cheeks heated. "Yes. Sorry. Everything's on the table, so we can eat." He pulled a chair out for Emilio and waited until he was seated before moving to his own chair.

Emilio picked up his fork and dug right in, moaning at the first taste of the food and making short work of cleaning his plate. Spencer smiled fondly and took a few bites, enjoying the show more than the meal. When Emilio peered down at his plate and frowned, apparently disappointed at the lack of food on it, Spencer chuckled.

"I have plenty more," he said. "Do you want seconds?"

The hopeful expression on Emilio's face had Spencer laughing outright.

"Yes," Emilio said, nodding furiously. "This is so good."

"No problem."

Spencer got up and took Emilio's plate into the kitchen, filled it to overflowing, and then returned it to Emilio's place mat. He set the plate down, returned to his chair, and watched Emilio resume the shoveling. It took Emilio a bit longer to polish off his plate this time, but he still managed to do it before Spencer finished his food.

"Ahh," he moaned, sounding wholly satisfied. He pushed his plate forward, leaned back in his chair, and rubbed his belly. "Damn, that was good." Now that the mad dash for food was over, Emilio focused on Spencer. His gaze dropped to Spencer's plate and he furrowed his brow. "Why ain't you eating?"

"I am eating!" Spencer said with a laugh. "I'm just going at it a bit...slower."

For the first time that day, Emilio's cheeks reddened. "Sorry," he said sheepishly. "I grew up with three brothers. If you didn't eat it fast, it was gone. I didn't mean to be rude after you worked so hard on this meal. Everything was delicious. You're a good cook."

"You weren't rude." Spencer set his fork down, deciding

he was comfortably full and didn't need to eat any more. "I'm flattered, actually. It means you really like it." He reached across the small table and set his hand down, palm up, then roamed his gaze over Emilio's exposed, muscular chest. "By the way," he said. "That's an interesting choice of dinner attire. Not that I'm complaining, mind you. I like the view."

Emilio tickled his fingers over Spencer's palm. "I was tryin' to impress you," he admitted easily. "I wanted to get you hot, but then I had to go and mess things up with my pig impression."

"You didn't mess anything up," Spencer assured him. Far from it. Seeing Emilio's toned chest and ripped abs close up had Spencer's dick ready to go again. It was hot and hard against his thigh and he reveled in the feeling of wanting, needing. He'd missed this. Well, as much as you could miss something you'd only ever had a taste of. Spencer dipped his chin and looked up at Emilio from underneath his lashes. "Your, uh, plan worked just fine."

"Oh ho! Is that right?" Emilio beamed, looking so proud. "Come over here." He patted his lap.

"Uh…" Spencer considered objecting and saying he was too old to sit on someone's lap. But he wanted to be closer to Emilio, wanted to feel those strong arms around him again. Refusing to do something he very much wanted due to some principle he didn't fully understand didn't make any sense, so Spencer got up and made his way around the table.

Just as soon as he was within arm's reach, Emilio yanked

him down so he was sitting on Emilio's lap, straddling his hips. "Hey," Emilio said as he circled his arms around Spencer's waist.

"Hi," Spencer answered. He propped his wrists on Emilio's broad shoulders and laced his fingers together behind Emilio's neck.

"You cooked, so I'm gonna clean up. Plus, I gotta fill you in on what I think you should do with your remodel," Emilio said. "But I was hopin' maybe we could make out a little first."

"Make out?" Spencer fidgeted and moaned when Emilio's thick erection pushed against his belly.

"Mmm hmm." Emilio moved his hand along Spencer's back, rucking up his shirt. "Just a little."

He urged Spencer forward until their lips connected and then licked his way into Spencer's mouth, giving him more of those amazing kisses. With Emilio's mouth tasting his, Emilio's hands petting him, and Emilio's big body enveloping his, Spencer relaxed into the moment. It felt good to be wanted, felt just as good to want, and Spencer didn't take for granted how lucky he was to be experiencing both feelings.

EMILIO SQUEEZED Spencer's knees and kept a firm grip on his legs as he pushed his hands up his thighs, massaging his muscles. "Mmm," he moaned into Spencer's mouth, taking kiss after kiss from soft, warm lips. "You feel good." One more kiss and then he moved his hand to the back of Spencer's head and rubbed his scalp. "Should we talk about your remodel now?"

Warm and pliable in his arms, Spencer rested his cheek on Emilio's shoulder and traced his nipple with one long finger. "You really don't have to do this," he said. "I mean, I'm grateful, but you work hard all day. You should be able to relax on a Friday night."

"Oh, I'm plenty relaxed," Emilio promised. "And I like what I do, so don't feel bad about letting me help out."

Spencer met Emilio's gaze and cupped his cheek. "Are you sure? Because I don't want to take advantage of you."

With his trademark crooked grin firmly in place, Emilio raised his eyebrows, gave Spencer his best leer, and said, "Baby, you can take advantage of me anytime."

Spencer snorted and lightly smacked his shoulder. "Cut it out, goofball!" he said, sounding happy and relaxed. Then he smiled and flashed his dimples, and Emilio felt warmed all the way through. He wanted more than anything to keep Spencer feeling exactly that way all the time.

"All right, so I think this house is in really good shape, all things considered. The floors need to be refinished; we already talked about that. A fresh coat of paint, inside and out, would do wonders. The layouts in the bathroom and kitchen aren't bad, but the fixtures are old, so you'll probably want to pull everything out and put in new cabinets and appliances and all that. The biggest issue is the electric. It hasn't ever been redone, nothing's up to code, and your electrical panel is too small. I'd start totally fresh there, rewire the whole house."

"Yeah," Spencer said with a nod. "That's pretty much what I was expecting. I have a good amount saved up, but not enough to do all of that yet. Do you think I should do it in parts or wait until I have enough money to do the whole project in one go?"

Without allowing himself even a moment to hesitate, Emilio barreled forward. "I think you do it all now. I can handle most of the labor myself, and what I can't do alone, my brothers can help with. A guy I know does cabinets, and he'll give you a good deal. Same on the fixtures. So that really just leaves the appliances as the big-ticket items."

"Wait." Spencer looked thoroughly confused. It was adorable. "You want this job? But I thought you already had a job working with your family business."

"I do have a job, but I start early, so I'm usually done by two and then I spend a few hours doing side work. I can work on your house in the afternoons and on weekends." Emilio took in a deep breath and tightened his grip on Spencer before putting the next part of his pitch on the table. "And instead of paying cash, we can work a trade. You let me move in here, feed me more of those great meals, and I'll cover the labor."

He was right to have increased his hold on Spencer,

because as soon as the offer registered, the man started wiggling, trying to get up off his lap.

"You can't do that!" Spencer blurted out.

"Sure I can. The biggest part of the job is electric, and I'm an electrician. It's a perfect fit," Emilio said with a wink.

"That's not what I meant."

"I know you're worried about the rest of it, but I'm a decent carpenter, I can lay tile, and for the type of work you need, I can do the plumbing. Did I mention that my dad started out as a plumber?"

"No." Spencer shook his head. "But that's not what—"

"And I'll be taking the general contractor's exam next year," Emilio said, pushing forward. "So I've been working alongside all the trades, making sure I have a full grasp of every aspect of construction, from foundation to roofing and everything in between. So you'll be in great hands, I promise."

"Emilio!" Spencer finally shouted.

"Yes, Spencer?" Emilio asked, using his best butter-wouldn't-melt-in-my-mouth tone.

Spencer narrowed his pretty brown eyes to tiny slits and glared at him. It was adorable, reminding him once again of the feral cats he had befriended as a child. He had to curl his lips in and bite them to keep from smiling.

"Don't act like you don't know what I mean. I cannot possibly let you do all that work without getting paid."

"I will be getting paid. Like I said, it's a trade—room and board in exchange for labor," Emilio said. Spencer opened his mouth, no doubt to object once again, but Emilio kept talking. "And actually, you'd be doing me a favor."

At that statement, Spencer slammed his mouth shut. "How would I be doing you a favor?" he asked.

"Well, right now I'm sharing a three-bedroom house with three other guys. Two have their own rooms, if you don't count the girls they have coming in and out of there, and I share with another guy. My one roommate has this girlfriend that's into being choked, and at least two nights a week I wake up because she's yelling at him to choke her harder while they're fucking. Between that and the beer cans everywhere and cars all over the lawn, which my other roommate keeps saying he's gonna fix up, and the pills the guy I share a room with swears are herbal but make him shake, and after he takes them, he sits around listening to music all night with his psychotic friend who only lets us call him the Horse, and we have to say the 'the' part or he loses his shit, I never get enough sleep, and I'm pretty sure any minute now we're gonna have an arson investigation on our hands." He took a deep breath and looked at Spencer's shocked face. "So you see? You really would be doing me a huge favor by letting me move in here and work on this remodel. What do you say?"

Spencer opened and closed his mouth a few times before answering. "I don't... I guess that does sound like a really bad situation you're in, and I would love to get started on the work, and I have the spare bedroom, so—"

"No," Emilio said. "The deal only applies if I sleep in your room. With you."

Spencer's eyes widened again and he started sputtering. "Are you saying you'll only work on my house if I have sex with you?" he asked, sounding positively scandalized.

Emilio gave a slow, sure nod, and said, "If that's what I need to do to stay in your bed. Oh yeah, that's exactly what I'm saying." Then he brushed his lips over Spencer's neck and whispered in his ear, "But don't worry, *cariño*, I'll make sure you like it." He moved his hand onto Spencer's lap and cupped and massaged his balls. When Spencer whimpered, Emilio grinned and pressed his advantage, saying, "So do we have a deal?"

With his breathing heavy and his arm trembling, Spencer tried to put his hand between them for a handshake. "I..." He gulped. "I guess, yeah, we do."

Emilio disregarded Spencer's hand and cupped his cheeks. "I already told you I ain't gonna shake your hand." He rubbed his thumbs along Spencer's jaw. "This ain't business. It's personal."

Though he still looked nervous, Spencer gripped Emilio's wrists and moved closer, making clear with his body language that he very much wanted a kiss. With a glow of victory radiating from him, Emilio bussed Spencer's lips. Spencer whimpered, the sound full of need, and Emilio felt an answering pang low in his belly.

"We better clean up now," Emilio said huskily. "'Cause if

STRONG ENOUGH                                    83

I keep on touching you, I'm gonna forget all about the dishes and go down on you right here in the kitchen."

"I can clean up later." Spencer was flushed and breathless. It was a good look on the man.

"No. You cooked. That means I clean up. That's how we did it in my family growing up."

Emilio loved the idea of carrying forward into this relationship what he'd learned from his parents. He already had such high hopes for where things could go with Spencer that, for a second, he had a flash of fear—what if he was wrong? What if he wouldn't be able to gain Spencer's trust? What if they weren't as compatible as he thought? But then he gazed into Spencer's eyes and recognized the same desires and needs he had, reflected right back at him. This man was different from anybody Emilio had met. Spencer was special, and, okay, yeah, he was scared, but he wanted this as much as Emilio. So just as fast as the uncharacteristic doubts hit him, they drained away.

"You go get ready for bed," he said tenderly. "I'll take care of things out here and then I'll come in and love on you."

# CHAPTER 7

FOLLOWING EMILIO'S directions in a daze, Spencer climbed off his lap and started walking out of the room. It had been the most surreal day of his life, and he couldn't quite get his bearings. But despite his seemingly constant sense of confusion, Spencer felt happy, really happy down deep. And he knew he owed that to Emilio.

Gorgeous Emilio, who had bartered sex with Spencer in exchange for construction services, which should had been offensive, really, and disconcerting in its similarity to prostitution, but Spencer found himself pleased beyond measure that Emilio wanted him that much.

Strong Emilio, who, instead of turning away in reaction to Spencer's hang-ups, had been patient, his arousal never flagging as he gave Spencer the best sexual experience he could remember.

Skilled Emilio, who would be able to bring Spencer's house into modern times almost by himself. Hopefully while shirtless and wearing a tool belt.

Kind Emilio, who was, at that very moment, clearing the table. Spencer came to a halt in the middle of the hall. It was rude to make his guest clean up and do the dishes, even if Emilio insisted. So Spencer turned around and walked back to the kitchen.

The sound of whistling stopped him in the doorway. He stood at the edge of the room and watched Emilio bop around as he picked up glasses, plates, and cutlery and carried them to the sink. He was smiling and literally whistling while he worked, looking happy as could be and seemingly feeling right at home. Spencer was amazed at how quickly Emilio had managed to assimilate into his home. The man fit perfectly.

He kept walking toward his target and took Emilio a bit off guard when he circled his arms around his waist, pressed his chest to Emilio's back, and squeezed him tight. "Hi," he mumbled against Emilio's smooth skin.

"Hey." After setting the bowl he was holding on the counter, Emilio shifted around so they were front to front, kissed his forehead, and combed his fingers through his hair. "Everything okay?"

Spencer blinked up at him. "This is weird, right?"

"Umm." Emilio furrowed his brow and said, "Explain what you mean."

"I don't know." He rested his head against Emilio's shoulder, avoiding eye contact but maintaining a physical connection. "This thing between us," he said. "It's kind of...a lot and it's really fast." He gulped and then looked up and met Emilio's eyes. "Isn't it?"

After stroking his hair for a few seconds, Emilio took in

a deep breath and said, "I really like being with you. It feels right to me. How about you? Are you happy about our plan, about me being here, being with you?"

"Yes," Spencer said before he could think too hard about it. Only a couple of minutes earlier, he had been thinking about how happy he felt. It would be mean to hold that back when Emilio was so open about his own feelings.

"Well, then, does it matter if it's weird? Yeah, it's fast, and yeah, it's different from what I'm used to, but you're happy, and I'm happy. Even if it's weird, what does it matter?"

Though it was a simplistic view of life or relationships or really just about anything, Spencer couldn't argue with it. He could probably come up with a million reasons to be anxious or to worry, but at its core, the situation came down to exactly what Emilio said—they were both happy. It was like he often explained to his students: the simple approach to solving a problem was usually the best one. No reason to complicate things.

"You're right." He traced Emilio's dark eyebrow with one finger. "I like the way you approach things, Emilio." He moved his finger around Emilio's full lips. "You have an amazing ability to ignore the noise and home in on the crux of an issue."

With a smile and a wink, Emilio said, "I have no clue what you just said, but thank you." Then he grasped Spencer's hand and held it in place as he licked and sucked on his finger.

"Ungh," Spencer moaned, pleasure hitting him fast, need

coming right after. He thrust his hips forward and Emilio reacted immediately, shoving his thickly muscled thigh between Spencer's legs and giving his rapidly filling dick something to rub against. Emilio's gaze burned as he fellated Spencer's finger, not stopping until Spencer was grinding hard and groaning loudly.

"You are so hot," Emilio whispered huskily when he finally popped his mouth off Spencer's finger. "I love how you react, love how real you are all the time." He slammed his lips against Spencer's and ate his way inside, thrusting his tongue in and out over and over again while he squeezed Spencer's ass. "Damn!" Emilio said as they broke for air. He held Spencer close and dropped his forehead onto Spencer's head. "I have no fuckin' control where you're concerned."

"That's not true," Spencer said hastily. "You were really controlled before when we were... You were great."

"Oh, *cariño*." Emilio cupped his cheeks and tilted his head back. His expression had changed and he suddenly looked sad. "I didn't mean it like that. I won't ever hurt you. I just meant that I want you so much all I can think about is getting you naked and going back to bed."

"Okay," Spencer responded breathlessly. "Let's do that. Is now okay?"

Emilio laughed. "See that? Cute as hell. How am I supposed to resist you?" He gave Spencer one last peck and then pulled away. "I gotta finish cleaning up. You better go, because if you stay in here, I won't be able to stop touching you and then I'll never finish these dishes."

"I'll wash them later." Spencer wrapped his hand around Emilio's and tried to tug him toward the doorway.

"No." Emilio didn't budge, and Spencer got a firsthand example of just how strong the man was. A shudder of arousal ran through his body. "You cooked, so I gotta clean up."

Something in Emilio's tone and the stubborn set of his shoulders told Spencer this was important. "Okay, but I want to help—that way it'll go faster. How about you wash and I'll dry?"

After a few seconds mulling it over, Emilio nodded and said, "That works."

"Great." Spencer beamed. "And we need to make sure a dishwasher is on the list for the kitchen remodel."

"No problem," Emilio said. "We have room right here." He tilted his chin toward a cabinet to his right. "We'll run the plumbing through the back and share a drain with the sink." He scrubbed plates and forks, put them in a soapy pile on one side of the wide sink, and then reached for more dishes as he said, "So tell me about your family."

"Oh, um, okay." Spencer wandered around the kitchen, putting away the few things he had left out when making dinner and wiping at invisible smudges on the countertop, anything to keep himself busy. "Let's see. My parents live in Orlando, which is where I grew up. My father is an engineer. My mother is a teacher. I have one brother. Steven. He's a banker, three years younger than me, also lives in Orlando. Divorced, two kids." He tried to think of what else he could say and realized he was all out of information about his family. Huh.

"Orlando is far," Emilio said.

"Yes," Spencer agreed. The answer was simple, the meaning behind it complicated. "But Vegas is a lot like Orlando, except with less humidity, and it's a little farther from the ocean. But I've never really been a beach guy, anyway, and California is close enough that I can drive there if the urge strikes."

"Yup," Emilio said with a chuckle. "It's a dry one ten. So we're burned to a crisp, but, hey, at least we're not being steamed."

They were talking about the weather. That wasn't usually considered an indication of a successful conversation. Even he knew that, and he was no expert at conversational skills.

"Spencer?" Emilio said after a too-long interlude of silence.

"Yes?"

"Is it hard being so far away from them or are you guys not close?"

Though Emilio was still facing the sink, his movements had slowed and his head was tilted a smidge to the side, so Spencer knew he was interested in the answer. It was actually easier to talk without being watched, something Emilio probably realized. In the short time he'd known the man, Spencer had already noticed how sensitive he was, how easily Emilio seemed to read him.

"Our relationship is…" Spencer tried to think of the right word to use and finally settled on, "Fine. Everybody is civil to each other, but they've made it clear they don't understand me, and everyone tends to be happier when we keep our distance." He shrugged. "I see them for a few days every couple of years, usually around a holiday."

"Does that bother you?" Emilio asked quietly, his tone almost soothing.

Spencer shrugged again, even though Emilio couldn't see him. "It isn't great," he admitted. After a deep breath, he added, "And I wish it could be different. But it can't."

"Why?" Emilio asked. "Do they have an issue with you being gay?"

"Yes and no," Spencer answered honestly. "I mean, coming out pointed out another difference between us, but I was never what they expected in a son." He swallowed hard and tried to sound nonchalant as he said, "It's no big deal. They have my brother and now grandkids. And I like it here."

Without saying a word or turning around, Emilio reached a soapy hand behind himself and held it out. The invitation was clear, and Spencer hesitated only a moment before taking it. He hurried over to the sink and threaded his fingers with Emilio's. Within seconds, he was tugged up against that broad, hard body and squeezed tightly.

"I'm sorry it's like that for you, *cariño*. Maybe it'll get better one day."

It wouldn't, and Spencer had long since stopped deluding himself by hoping otherwise, but he didn't say that, partly because he didn't want to sound bitter and partly because, despite his maturity, Emilio was still really young and the last thing Spencer wanted to do was jade him.

After letting himself enjoy the warmth and strength of Emilio's embrace for a bit longer, Spencer stepped back and said, "Are you ready for me to dry?"

Thankfully, Emilio didn't press the topic further. He turned the handle on the faucet and started rinsing off suds before handing the wet dishes to Spencer. They worked together companionably, and by the time they were done, Spencer was no longer thinking about the loss of his family and was instead thinking about how nice it was to share simple everyday tasks with Emilio.

"Emilio?"

"Uh-huh?" Emilio handed Spencer the last glass, turned off the water, and dried his hands with a towel as he turned around.

"How long do you think the remodeling project will take?"

"Why?" Emilio asked, his eyes sparkling and his lips tilted upward in a wicked grin. "Are you already in a rush to get me out of here?"

"No," Spencer responded right away.

"Good answer, *cariño*." Emilio swept him into his arms

once again and kissed his cheek. "Good answer."

EMILIO GAZED into Spencer's warm, brown eyes and felt as much as heard the man's breath quicken. He smirked and puffed out his chest a little. His ego was healthy enough to get off on that reaction, on how quickly and easily he could ramp up the smart, successful older man.

"You ready to go back to bed?" he asked, keeping his voice low. Then he licked his lips.

"Mmm hmm," Spencer said as he bobbed his head, his gaze locked on Emilio's mouth.

"Damn, you're sweet," Emilio rasped.

"Huh?" Spencer slowly dragged his eyes up to meet Emilio's.

"You like my mouth?" he asked sensually as he dipped his head down so his breath ghosted over Spencer's skin. "Want to feel it all over your body?" He trailed his fingers over Spencer's shoulders, his arms, his chest, and his belly, making Spencer whimper. "Think I can make you come that way?" He ran one finger from the head of Spencer's engorged cock to the root. "Or do you want me to suck you?"

Spencer grabbed Emilio's shoulders and bucked forward as he cried out. "Emilio?" he panted. "I've never—" Emilio moved his finger up the length of Spencer's shaft and the rest of Spencer's sentence garbled as his eyes rolled back in his head.

"What's that?" he whispered. "I don't think I heard you."

"God," Spencer whispered, his eyes still closed. "You make me feel so much." He blinked his eyes open. "Please," he begged. "Don't tease me. It's not ever like this for me, just..." He gulped and pierced Emilio with his stare. "Please don't tease me."

Filling the man with desire was one thing, but terrifying him in the process was quite another. "Hey," Emilio said softly as he gathered Spencer in his arms and cuddled him close. "I ain't teasing you. I'm gonna make you feel so good." He dragged his stubble over Spencer's smooth cheek. "Let's go to bed so I can show you."

They started walking toward the bedroom, Emilio's arm around Spencer's shoulders, and then Spencer halted and turned to face Emilio. "What about you?" he asked.

"Uh, what do you mean?" Emilio furrowed his brow in confusion.

"You said you're going to make me feel good. But what about you? What are you getting out of it?"

"You're kidding, right?" Emilio snorted. Spencer dropped his chin to his chest and his shoulders drooped. Damn it. "Hey, now," Emilio said. "That came out wrong. I'm sorry, it's just..." He put two fingers under Spencer's chin and raised it until their eyes met. "You have got to realize by now that I want you. A lot. You do it for me, Spencer. Have since the first time I saw you. So you better believe I'm getting something out of this. Touching you, tasting you, hearing you..." He shuddered at those thoughts. "I'm gonna feel as good as you. Believe me."

"Yeah?"

He took Spencer's hand and placed it over his swollen shaft. "Oh, yeah," he promised.

"And..." Spencer swallowed hard. "You'll tell me if I don't... If it's not right, you'll tell me? Because I can fix it if I know it's not good. I can..." He looked into Emilio's eyes and pleaded, "Please tell me if I'm not... Because I want to make you feel good too, Emilio. I want that so much."

Somebody had fucked with Spencer's mind as well as his body, Emilio realized. He clenched his fists so tightly his knuckles cracked.

"Being with you feels good," he said, trying to reassure Spencer.

"But you'll tell me, right?" Spencer clutched Emilio's forearms. "If it isn't good, you'll tell me?"

Though he knew it wouldn't be an issue given his powerful reaction to Spencer, Emilio realized the only way to address this particular worry was to give Spencer the oath he wanted, so he said, "Yes, I'll tell you. I promise."

"Okay," Spencer said, sounding relieved.

"Okay." Emilio smiled. "Are we done talking now? 'Cause I'm ready to do dirty things to you."

"Dirty?" Spencer asked, already sounding breathless.

"Uh-huh," Emilio answered as he pulled Spencer toward the bedroom. "Maybe even illegal."

Spencer whimpered and hurried his pace. As soon as they entered the bedroom, Emilio pushed his shorts down over his hips and let them drop to the ground, leaving him stark naked. Spencer froze, arms hanging by his sides, mouth open, eyes wide.

Emilio chuckled and raised Spencer's chin with one finger, closing his mouth. "Like what you see?" he asked as he wrapped his long fingers around his thick shaft and stroked slowly.

"God." Spencer licked his lips and gulped. He flicked his gaze up to Emilio's. "You're beautiful."

"I'm glad you think so," Emilio said, running his free hand over his belly and chest while he continued to pump his cock.

"No, really." Spencer dragged his eyes from Emilio's face to his feet and back up again. "I've never seen anybody who looks like you."

"I like looking at you too," Emilio said. He reached for the bottom of Spencer's shirt. "Let's take this off, okay? I wanna see you naked."

Though he seemed nervous, Spencer complied, raising his arms above his head when Emilio pulled his shirt up and shoving his briefs and jeans to the ground as soon as Emilio unbuttoned them. Emilio rested his palm over Spencer's heart and felt the rapid beat.

"I won't hurt you," he promised.

Spencer took in a deep breath and said, "I know." He shook his head ruefully. "Which is crazy because we just met, but I know you won't hurt me."

"That's good, *cariño*," he said.

He led them over to the bed and lay back, pulling Spencer down on top of him and groaning when their exposed skin met. Spencer gazed at him, his eyes filled with so much hope it made Emilio want to give him whatever he had been missing. The more he got to know Spencer, the more he realized there was so much left to learn about him. One thing he knew with certainty was that Spencer had been hurt more than once in his life by people he had trusted. Letting down a man with that kind of past could cause a lot of damage.

When he was standing in Spencer's kitchen washing dishes, Emilio had taken stock of himself and considered whether this was a man he should pursue. Barreling ahead only to walk away if things got hard would be unfair and cruel, especially to someone with Spencer's past. But just the sound of Spencer's voice trying to sound upbeat when discussing his family had put a vise on Emilio's heart, making him itch to touch and soothe the other man, so he knew he couldn't walk away. He wanted Spencer in a way he had never wanted another, and there was no way he could give that up.

After less than a day, Spencer was sharing information about his family and welcoming Emilio's touch. Emilio figured that meant he was doing something right and that, maybe, building a relationship with Spencer wouldn't be as hard as he had initially feared. Thankfully, whatever challenges lay ahead, convincing Spencer to want him wasn't one of them. He just had to work on gaining Spencer's trust, his complete trust, and then maybe he'd be invited to stay in Spencer's life long after he finished the remodel.

# CHAPTER 8

SPENCER LAY on top of Emilio and enjoyed the feeling of hard muscle and hot flesh beneath him. The big man lay still as Spencer traced his eyebrows, the perimeter of his ear, and the bridge of his nose. In this position, Spencer held the control, so it was easier to follow his instincts and take chances. First and foremost, that meant indulging in more of those spine-melting kisses, so he slowly lowered his face and brushed his lips against Emilio's.

"Mmm." Emilio sighed and closed his eyes in response to the light touch. He opened his lips and stretched his neck, looking like a baby bird as he searched for more kisses.

Spencer smiled and lapped at the full red lips, chuckling when Emilio's eyes fluttered open in surprise. "You taste good," he said by way of explanation.

"Oh yeah?" Emilio chuckled. "You gonna check if that applies all over?" He thrust his hips up, nudging Spencer with his erection as he waggled his eyebrows.

Spencer felt a pull in his groin in response to that suggestion. "Yes," he said, his voice sounding rough with arousal.

Before Spencer could make good on that promise, Emilio cupped his nape and pulled him down for more kisses. They tilted in concert, finding the perfect angle, and then nipped and licked each other until, eventually, Emilio darted his tongue into Spencer's mouth, petting his tongue and mingling their flavors together.

"I love kissing you," Spencer confessed.

"So don't stop. Keep kissing me." Emilio wrapped his strong arms around Spencer and caressed his back and ass.

"Yeah? You don't mind? I mean, I know you wanted to..." Spencer let the sentence trail off, still feeling bashful about speaking the words. He knew the drill, though. Sex was about orgasms. A little bit of foreplay was okay, but demanding too much was a surefire way to leave someone feeling frustrated and make them lose interest.

"We'll get to that," Emilio responded. "We're not in a rush. It's still early. We've already eaten dinner. We don't have work in the morning. Keep kissing me. I like it too."

Still feeling like he was in a dream leaps and bounds better than any of his fantasies, Spencer bent down and tentatively touched his lips to Emilio's once again. When Emilio swiped his tongue over Spencer's lips and continued holding him close, he set aside his concerns and fell into the kiss. As their mouths moved together, Spencer rocked his hips against Emilio's stomach and tangled his fingers in silky black hair.

He lost track of time as they touched and kissed. It was

so good, so right, he felt sorry for everybody who missed this, everybody who rushed to the end and skipped the pleasure of the journey. And he might have stayed where he was, licking and nuzzling and kissing Emilio's now swollen mouth, but he wiggled a little and the wet tip of Emilio's cock brushed against his erection.

"Oh!" he groaned into Emilio's mouth and reached between them, skating his palm over the burning shaft.

His mouth watered at the thought of how Emilio's seed would taste, and he no longer wanted to wait to find out. With one last peck to Emilio's lips, Spencer nibbled his way down Emilio's throat, lapped at Emilio's right nipple, and wriggled down the bed until he was looking right at Emilio's thick dick.

"God," he said huskily and then gulped to swallow down the thickness in his throat. He darted his tongue out and took his first taste of the moisture leaking from the flared crown.

"Ungh, fuck!" Emilio shouted and bucked up. He combed his fingers through Spencer's hair and rubbed his scalp. "I'm already so close," he rasped. "It won't take long."

Spencer flattened his tongue and swiped it over Emilio's big balls and up his hard cock, then he flicked his tongue back and forth over the slit. Emilio's muscles went taut, his breathing quickened, and he clutched the bedsheet tightly. Cupping Emilio's full balls in one hand and stroking his thick cock with the other, Spencer looked up and met Emilio's gaze as he dropped his lips over the ruddy glans and sucked hard.

"Spence!" Emilio cried out. He gasped for air and humped

upward. "Oh, Jesus. Oh, Jesus," he panted. "I'm gonna." His eyes rolled back in his head and he made a deep keening sound. "You gotta move," he warned.

And, normally, Spencer would have done exactly that, but not at that moment, not with this man. Instead, he moaned in pleasure and sucked harder. That seemed to be the breaking point for Emilio, who opened his mouth on a silent scream as he shook and pulsed long streams of ejaculate onto Spencer's waiting tongue.

Spencer was still licking when Emilio hunched over, put a hand under each of his arms, and yanked him up. "Thank you," he whispered against Spencer's mouth. He tangled his left hand in Spencer's hair and rubbed his waist with the other. "So good," he said as he brushed his lips over Spencer's. He pushed his right knee between Spencer's legs, putting delicious pressure on his balls, as he rolled them to their sides, all while continuing the light kisses.

Though he was achingly hard, Spencer was in no rush to do anything about it. After going so long without that feeling, he reveled in it. So he returned Emilio's kisses, mapped his muscular back with his palms, and slowly rocked against his thick thigh, keeping himself primed but not quite ready to blow.

Many minutes later, after one particularly intense kiss, Emilio hoarsely said, "I can taste myself in your mouth." He licked his way into Spencer's mouth and sucked on his tongue. "That is so hot." He ran his finger down Spencer's forehead, over his nose, then his lips, and finally his chin. "I know I said I was gonna seduce you, but then you were naked and we were touching and kissing and…" Emilio took a deep breath and shrugged sheepishly. "I'm sorry for getting distracted and going off course. You're pretty irresistible."

"That's okay," Spencer said. "I enjoyed the side trip."

Emilio circled his fingers around Spencer's dick and gave it a light squeeze. "I can see that," he said. He rolled his hips and dragged his renewed erection over Spencer's balls.

"Already?" Spencer asked with a chuckle. "What's it been, ten minutes? Maybe fifteen?"

"I recharge fast," Emilio confirmed.

*Ah, to be twenty-two again.* Spencer grinned inwardly as he leaned forward and kissed Emilio, reached for his dick, and then pumped it in time with Emilio's thrusting tongue.

"Ungh, Spence!" Emilio cried out. "That feels good, but you gotta stop."

Spencer didn't want to stop. He wanted to keep touching Emilio's amazing body, to indulge in more of his passionate kisses, to watch Emilio come apart at his touch. When he didn't pull away, Emilio rolled him onto his back and peeled Spencer's hand off his dick. He snapped his gaze to Emilio's.

"What… Did I do something wro—"

"You're amazing." Emilio brought Spencer's hand to his mouth and kissed it. "But if you keep touching me like that, I'm gonna lose it again. Before that happens, I gotta get your pretty dick in my mouth."

Hearing those words left Spencer speechless and gasping for air. He whimpered, and Emilio grinned then moved down his body and wedged himself between Spencer's legs. "Open for me, *cariño*," he said as he knelt between Spencer's thighs.

Spencer forced himself to remain loose and pliant as Emilio spread his knees and pushed them up and out. It felt awkward to be so exposed; Spencer had to fight to keep from covering his groin with his hands and clapping his knees together. But then Emilio nuzzled and lapped at his sac and moaned happily, distracting Spencer from his embarrassment. He looked down and watched as the most gorgeous man he had ever seen used his mouth to give him more pleasure than he'd ever thought possible.

"You smell so good," Emilio mumbled as he buried his face in the juncture between Spencer's thigh and groin, sniffing and then sucking on his skin. "Taste amazing too." He grasped each side of Spencer's ass with a large hand and kneaded.

Dizzy from the arousal evoked by Emilio's words and touch, Spencer was slow to realize that his ass was being spread open and rolled up. Without a warning, Emilio buried his face in Spencer's cleft and mouthed his sensitive skin, opening and closing his lips, sucking and licking and damn near eating Spencer's ass.

"Emilio!" Spencer shouted.

Though he didn't stop his oral ministrations, Emilio looked up and met Spencer's gaze. It was dirtier and hotter in equal measures—looking into Emilio's eyes as he swiped his tongue over Spencer's pucker. He pushed Spencer's knees up and said, "Hold on to them."

With a gulp, Spencer complied, clasping the underside of his knees and holding his legs close to his chest. "Like...like this?" he asked, feeling his face heat.

"Oh, yeah," Emilio said reverently as he caressed Spencer's belly, his thighs, and his ass. "Just like that." Then he fisted Spencer's dick and dropped more openmouthed kisses in his cleft.

"Oh...oh...oh," Spencer whimpered as he lay in his bed, holding himself open and watching Emilio ravish him.

His noises melded with Emilio's almost constant grunts and groans, and the bed shook from Emilio's movements as he humped the mattress. When Emilio reached for his own dick and then moved both of his hands at the same rapid pace, stroking off Spencer while he fisted himself, Spencer knew he was nearing the end.

"Close," he whispered hoarsely.

Emilio responded by pointing his tongue and poking it in and out of Spencer's ass over and over again, all the while continuing to jack Spencer's dick. Sooner than he would have liked, Spencer's orgasm curled low in his groin. He rolled his shoulders off the bed and clutched Emilio's forearm, needing to hold on to him so he wouldn't fly apart.

After a final push of his tongue into Spencer's body and another long swipe across Spencer's channel, Emilio rose to his knees, his dick in his left hand and Spencer's in his right. "Come on, come on, come on," he chanted as he stroked and thrust his hips back and forth, simulating an act Spencer suddenly craved.

With that thought in mind, Spencer's entire body stiffened and he cried out Emilio's name as he shot hard, jets of creamy white semen covering his belly and drizzling over Emilio's fingers.

"Yes!" Emilio shouted. He leaned over Spencer's body and gave himself three more strokes before he came, adding more liquid heat to Spencer's skin. He didn't stop pumping until they were both drained, and then he dropped his forehead onto Spencer's chest, remaining crouched above him as he sucked in air.

With a trembling hand, Spencer petted Emilio's hair as he caught his breath. It was combustible, this thing between them, unlike anything he'd previously experienced. Their chemistry together was off the charts, filling Spencer with a deep sense of pride. Then he had a disconcerting thought.

"Emilio?" he asked hesitantly.

Emilio kissed his sternum and then raised his gaze. "Yes?"

"Is it always like this for you? When you...with other guys, is it always so..."

"Never." Emilio shook his head. "Only with you, Spencer," he said, sounding almost awed. "You're incredible."

The praise filled him with pride and satisfaction. He

reached for Emilio and tugged, urging him up. "Can we kiss more?" he asked, feeling uncharacteristically bold.

"Always." Emilio kissed his hand and then scooted up so they were face-to-face again. Then he rolled them onto their sides and drew Spencer close. "Love kissing you, *cariño*."

BECAUSE HE had to be up by five on weekdays to get to the job site on time, Emilio generally went to bed by nine. If he wanted to go out on a Friday night, he'd catch a nap after work, knowing it was the only way to stay awake late enough to have a good time. But that night, when the clock ticked past eleven, he was still awake, watching Spencer sleep in his arms.

He smoothed his palm over Spencer's hair and looked at him in wonder. His immediate attraction to the older man hadn't surprised him. Emilio had always preferred guys with more life under their belts, a bit of salt with the pepper, the sides of their eyes crinkling when they smiled. Plus, though he had a big, muscular build by nature, from his work, and because he devoted time to staying in shape, he had no interest in taking someone with his own body type to bed. Instead, he was attracted to men who were smaller and softer. So as far as physical types went, Spencer hit the mark in every way.

Having worked alongside his parents and siblings for as long as he could remember, he needed to be with someone who recognized the importance of a steady job more than the next party. And he respected a guy who worked hard and saved for things that mattered, like improving his house. Having been raised by a father who took immense pride in being the first in his family to buy his own home, and who drove his truck into the ground before he replaced it, Emilio had a hard time connecting with guys whose closets were overflowing with designer clothes yet they never had enough money to buy their own drinks. And during the past year, he had gone out with at least three men who lived in tiny shared apartments, yet drove the latest BMW. Though Spencer's family sounded completely different from his own, it seemed that they valued the same things.

Plus he had to admit, there was something satisfying about being needed, and Spencer called to every one of his protective instincts. The way Spencer looked at him, wide-eyed and reverent, made Emilio feel like he was ten feet tall and powerful enough to do anything. The man was a rare mix of mature responsibility and sweet shyness, so no wonder Emilio was drawn to him.

But even though Spencer's appearance hit all his buttons and even though he respected Spencer's career and ethics and had enjoyed hanging out with him more than he had enjoyed spending time with someone in as long as he could remember, Emilio was still blindsided by how he had felt once they got in bed. His first sexual experience had been at seventeen, fumbling hurriedly with another boy from school. It hadn't taken long for things to escalate, and by eighteen, he was out of his parents' house and getting laid regularly. Emilio considered himself pretty experienced when it came to sex and thought that, other than some seriously kinky shit he had no interest in trying, he had done what there was to do and felt what there was to feel.

One day with Spencer had proven him wrong. Nobody had ever made him feel so good, so alive, so full of desire. Just remembering the wet heat of Spencer's mouth on his dick and the scent, taste, and feel of Spencer's silky skin when Emilio rimmed him made his balls ache and his cock plump back up again. Taking in a deep breath, Emilio tightened his hold on Spencer.

"You're amazing," he whispered.

Spencer made a muffled sound and shifted. Emilio stayed still, hoping he hadn't woken him, but then his eyelids fluttered open. "You're really here," he mumbled, giving him a sleepy smile. "I was sure it was all a dream." He kneaded Emilio's chest with long fingers.

"Not a dream," Emilio said with a chuckle. "But I can understand why you thought so. What we did in this bed was the stuff of fantasies."

"My fantasies have never been that good," Spencer confessed, his voice thick with sleep.

Emilio snorted and said, "Yeah, I guess mine haven't

either." He dropped a kiss onto Spencer's forehead and rubbed circles on his back. "Sorry I woke you up. I didn't know I was being loud. You go back to sleep, okay?"

"You didn't wake me up," Spencer responded. "At least I don't think you did." He rubbed his eyes and then settled his gaze on Emilio. "What do you mean loud? And why're you awake? What time is it?"

"Damn, but are you adorable." Emilio shook his head in wonder. "It's a little after eleven. And I was about to close my eyes, but I wanted to look at you for a little longer."

"You were looking at me?"

It was too dark to make out any details, but Emilio would have bet good money that Spencer was blushing.

"Yeah, *cariño*. I like looking at you."

Spencer ran his hand over the side of Emilio's face. "I've never been with anyone like you," he whispered.

"No?" Emilio paused and considered whether he should push for information. He wanted to know more about Spencer's past, and half-asleep, the man's guard was down. Hoping he wasn't taking advantage, he said, "What kinds of guys have you been with?"

"Not as nice as you," Spencer said as he moved his hand over Emilio's belly.

"They weren't nice to you?"

Spencer shrugged like it was no big deal. "They were okay, but you're..." He gazed at Emilio like he was something amazing and special, making Emilio yearn to live up to that expectation. "Nobody is like you," he ended on a whisper. After a few seconds of silence, with Emilio petting Spencer's hair and Spencer tracing his finger over Emilio's nipples, Spencer blinked at him and said, "I won't hold it against you if you change your mind."

"Change my mind?"

"Yes. About doing all this work on my house for free." Spencer lowered his gaze. "If you decide I'm not worth it, I'll understand."

That answer hit Emilio like a kick to his chest, leaving him a little out of breath. He wanted to punch whoever had made this handsome, tender, smart man think so little of himself. "Anybody who can't see that being with you is worth a little work is an idiot," he growled.

Spencer dropped a kiss on his chest and gave him a quick squeeze. "Have you ever lived with someone before?" he asked.

"My family, then roommates, but no, not like you mean." He put his finger under Spencer's chin and raised it so their eyes met. "Not like it's gonna be with you. What about you?"

"I lived with a boyfriend once, almost ten years ago. That's what first brought me to Vegas, actually. We met in Chicago, and about six months after we started dating, Chad got a job at Motorola here. There was a position at UNLV so I applied and we moved together."

It was unreasonable to be jealous of someone Spencer had dated before they'd met. Hell, Emilio had been in middle school ten years earlier. So it was ridiculous to harbor any sort of jealousy or anger about the fact that someone else had lived with Spencer, touched Spencer, kissed Spencer. Emilio shook off those thoughts and concentrated on the task at hand: getting to know the man who was now *his*.

"And then what happened?" Emilio asked.

"He didn't like his job, didn't like Vegas, so he decided to move back to Chicago."

When Spencer didn't explain further, Emilio realized he would have to nudge him along in order to keep the conversation going. "You didn't want to go with him?" he asked.

"He didn't ask me to."

"You mean he moved you here and then left you?" Emilio asked angrily, and then he reminded himself the story was about something that had happened a long time ago. Plus, if Spencer's ex had been more decent, Emilio wouldn't now have a chance with him, so he should be grateful for whatever happened. But it was hard to feel grateful about something that must have been painful for Spencer.

"Yes, but things weren't great between us, so I didn't expect him to. Besides, I like living here. I love my job. I have some great friends. I'm fine with how things turned out."

"And you haven't wanted to live with anybody again?"

"No." Spencer shook his head. "I've had a few boyfriends, but nobody serious enough to live together." He sighed. "Emilio, I'm pretty boring. I teach math. I don't go out much unless it's to dinner or brunch with friends. A great evening for me is experimenting with a new recipe and lying on the couch reading a new book."

"That sounds perfect," Emilio said excitedly.

"Seriously?"

"Oh yeah. I love your cooking, and I saw your couch—there's room for two on there if we snuggle close, and it's in front of the TV. Would it bother you if I watch a game or something while you're reading?"

Spencer stared at him for many long seconds, looking completely bewildered. "You're planning our evenings?"

"Well, yeah. I'm moving in here so we can spend time together. Works out great that we like the same things, huh?"

Instead of answering his question, Spencer asked, "Don't you think this is all moving a little fast?"

"Fast for who?"

"I don't know." Spencer furrowed his brow in confusion. "Faster than how people do things. We *just* met."

"Yeah, well, I got you interested and I ain't takin' the chance of someone else coming in and stealing you from me. I don't know what happened with those ex-boyfriends of yours, but I can see a good thing when he's lying naked next to me." Emilio grinned and winked. "This is my shot at you, Spencer, and I ain't gonna blow it like those other guys." He paused and then smirked as he said, "I'll blow you, though. Anytime you want."

# CHAPTER 9

WHEN SPENCER walked into his office building on Monday morning, he felt like he had been gone for two months instead of two days. He wasn't a man who embraced change easily; it took him weeks to adjust to a new set of towels or different placement of the cleaning supplies under his kitchen sink. But between the end of his workday on Friday and the start of the day on Monday, everything in his home and his personal life had changed.

Well, maybe not everything, because Emilio didn't have all that much stuff, so other than the bedroom closet and a few things in the bathroom, Spencer's house looked mostly the same. But that was only if you were skimming the surface. Underneath there was a huge difference: another man lived in his house. *Emilio Sanchez* lived in his house. And he'd soon be starting construction—refinishing the floors, remodeling the bathroom and kitchen, redoing the electrical system.

In his entire life, Spencer had never been impetuous, had never moved quickly to change anything, had never blindly jumped with both feet into something that mattered, or even something that didn't. But no amount of trepidation, or even abject fear, was going to keep him from pursuing a relationship with Emilio. Given the number of dead-end relationships he had been part of or witnessed in his almost four decades, he knew a guy like Emilio—sweet, sexy, talented, attentive—was rare. So if Emilio was willing to give him the time of day, Spencer would push himself outside of his comfort zone. The time spent with Emilio would be worth it, even if the man ultimately decided not to pursue a future together.

"Dr. Derdinger! Dr. Derdinger!"

He stopped at the sound of the panicked voice and looked back over his shoulder to see one of the students from his complex variables class running down the hallway. One week into the fall semester, he hadn't yet memorized every student's name, and just placing the young man's particular class seemed like cause for a pat on the back.

He waited for the student to catch up, then shifted his hold on his briefcase and said, "What can I do for you?"

"Oh, I uh..." The man panted, both hands on his knees, and tried to catch his breath. "Sorry," he said, sounding winded. "I shouldn't have run after you like that." A few more gasps. "Asthma."

Spencer frowned in concern and said, "Do you have an inhaler?"

Floppy blond hair bobbed, and the student slipped his backpack off his shoulders and started fumbling with the zipper on the front pocket.

"I have it," Spencer said as he dropped to his knees, let go of his briefcase, and reached for the man's backpack. He located the inhaler and handed it over. After a couple of puffs and some more deep breathing, the man sounded better. Spencer put his hand on a bony shoulder and said, "Are you okay?"

"Yeah." The young man squeezed his eyes shut. "Just embarrassed. Sorry." He opened his big blue eyes and looked at Spencer from underneath his lashes.

"Don't worry about it." Spencer gave his shoulder a squeeze and then gathered his briefcase and the backpack and stood up. "My office is a few doors down, and I have comfortable chairs. Are you okay to walk?"

With a nod and another breath, the man straightened. They stayed silent as they walked to Spencer's office. Spencer listened closely to the pace of his student's breaths and focused on whether he sounded better.

"I need you to tell me if I should call for help or take you to the student clinic, okay? That doctor title is for a PhD, not an MD. You don't want to be stuck with me if you have medical needs."

He unlocked his office door and pushed it open, then waited for his student to walk in before following him inside.

"I'm okay," the man said as he settled into the chair. "Promise. This happens sometimes." He dipped his chin. "I saw you walking into the building from across the plaza and I wanted to catch you, but the pollen count's probably high and I should've known better. I'm sorry about that."

"Stop apologizing. It wasn't a big deal." Spencer set the backpack down next to the student's feet, then walked behind his desk, put his briefcase on it, and sat down. "I believe you're in my complex variables class. What can I do for you?"

That pale skin hid nothing, and at that moment a red haze was climbing up the flushed neck, making Spencer worry that maybe his student wasn't as fine as he claimed.

"Yeah, that's right. My name's Abraham Green. Abe. And, uh, my question isn't about class exactly."

"Oh?"

Abe gulped. "You're gay, right? That's what I heard."

The question was completely unexpected and left Spencer momentarily stunned. Once he snapped out of it, he immediately darted his gaze to his door and relaxed when he saw it was open. The last thing he needed was to deal with false accusations.

When Spencer didn't respond to his question, Abe's eyes widened and he started stammering. "Oh, God. That came out all wrong. It's none of my business, but I want to go into teaching and I'm gay, so I was worried about job prospects. I was talking about it to my friend who had you last year. She's the one who recommended your class. She said you're one of the few profs in the department who actually makes sense." His words were coming out faster and faster, and his breathing quickened. "Anyway, she said you were gay and you teach so you might know, and I didn't have anybody else to talk to and—"

"Abe," Spencer said, cutting off the young man before he started wheezing again. "It's fine. Keep calm, okay?"

He smiled, hoping it came across as comforting. Understanding the reason for the question quelled his discomfort. Though he didn't know how he felt about the fact that his personal life was something being discussed by his students, he had never hidden being gay, having brought boyfriends to the department functions he occasionally had to attend. Helping students talk through career choices was a fairly common part of his job, even if the reason for this particular question was out of the ordinary.

"All right," he said when Abe seemed less panicky. "Let's try this again. You want to teach?"

"Yes." Abe nodded. "High school or maybe middle school. Math, obviously, 'cause it's my major. Dual major, actually. Math and education."

"Right." Spencer leaned forward, propped his arms on his desk, and clasped his hands together. "Teaching kids is different than teaching at the college level. But I know people who are out, and they work in town at all different grade levels, from second grade to high school. You might have to deal with the occasional jerk, and you'll need to be more careful than the female teachers to avoid even the appearance of impropriety, but from what I know, there are several districts where being gay isn't going to keep you out of the classroom."

Abe sighed in relief. "Thank you, Dr. Derdinger. That's what I thought, but when I came out this summer, all I heard from my father was that he had wasted money on three years of school because I'd never be able to get a job working with children." He paused and blinked rapidly. "I figured it wouldn't be like that, but my stepmother is a teacher in Utah, so I thought maybe he was right."

Fifteen years crumpled into nothing, and Spencer remembered exactly how he'd felt when he had come out to his family and faced a wall of rejection. "Oh, Abe. I'm sorry." He pushed his chair back, got up, and walked toward his student. "Your father is wrong. I'm sure you'll make a great teacher."

He hadn't quite turned the corner around his desk when Abe leaped out of his chair and up against Spencer, wrapping scrawny arms around him and burying his face in Spencer's shoulder. Abe's body shook for a couple of minutes, but eventually he got himself under control. He lifted his face and looked at Spencer with wet, red-rimmed eyes. "I, uh, thank you," he said. "I'm sorry."

"No more apologies. And you're welcome. I've been where you are and I know it's hard." Always practical, Spencer moved on to the nuts and bolts of Abe's situation. "Are you going to be okay with school? Is your father cutting you off?"

"Ha!" Abe barked a satisfied little laugh. "He wanted to, but when I told my mom about it, she called him and reminded him about their divorce decree. Turns out he's legally obligated to pay for college." He waggled his thin, light eyebrows. "My mom married her divorce lawyer, so trying to get out of it would cost my dad a bunch of money. He paid for the whole year, but I haven't heard from him since."

"Nice." Spencer chuckled. "Your mom sounds great. Things are still okay with her?"

"Yeah." Abe nodded. "She's already joined PFLAG, and she's dragging my stepdad to meetings. It's only my dad who's acting like an asshole." Abe shrugged. "Whatever. I don't care."

Spencer knew from personal experience the assertion wasn't completely true, but he also knew that sometimes it was the only thing you could do to protect yourself. He rubbed his hands up and down Abe's arms and thought about anything else he could say to help the young man work through what was obviously a difficult time, when a knock on his open door startled him.

He darted his gaze over to the doorway and was surprised to see Emilio standing there, glowering.

"Am I interrupting something?" Emilio asked.

AFTER THE weekend he had shared with Spencer, the last thing Emilio expected was to walk in on him with another man. His head was swimming, trying to process what he was seeing, and his body was fighting itself on whether to run away or dash inside and use force to remove the small blond from Spencer. Without his conscious permission, he settled on staying where he was and knocking.

"Emilio!" Spencer said happily, which started taming the fire in his belly. He stepped away from the man he had been hugging and reached his hand out to Emilio. There, that felt better. "Come in," he said. "This is one of my students, Abraham Green." He pointed at the other man. "Abe, this is—"

Emilio strode in, wrapped his left arm around Spencer's shoulders possessively, and tugged him close. "Emilio Sanchez. Spencer's boyfriend." He puffed his chest, trying to look intimidating as he held his right hand out.

"Oh, wow." The man's blue eyes widened. He put his smaller hand in Emilio's and shook it as he glanced over at Spencer. "Wow," he said again.

Spencer chuckled and said, "Tell me about it."

"So, uh, okay, yeah." Abe skittered over to his backpack, flung it on his shoulder, and made a beeline toward the door. "Thanks for the advice, Dr. D. See you in class." He slammed the door behind him as he ran out.

Emilio glared at the door.

"This is a nice surprise," Spencer said, drawing his attention. "I didn't realize you were going to be working on campus today. I thought I'd have to wait until tonight to see you."

"Is that why he was here?" Emilio asked before he could stop himself, and then he winced internally at how stupidly jealous he probably sounded.

"What do you mean?" Spencer looked genuinely confused. "Wait." His expression turned to shock. "Are you... You're not jealous of my student, are you?"

Emilio flopped down into the chair across from Spencer's desk. "Maybe a little." He paused and thought about brushing it off, saying it wasn't a big deal, but he knew himself well enough to realize if he did that, what he'd seen would continue to eat at him until he exploded and demanded an answer. Might as well skip the dramatics and get to it now. "Is there something going on with you two?"

Spencer gaped. "You can't be serious." When Emilio kept his steady gaze on him, he raised his eyebrows and said, "Okay, so you're serious, but come on. I don't know how you could think that. He's my student and he's just a kid."

"Just a kid, huh?" Emilio raised his eyebrows and looked at Spencer meaningfully.

"Yes! He's an undergrad. He's not even graduating until May, which means he's..." Spencer paused. "Twenty-one, twenty-two at the oldest."

Honestly, for an incredibly intelligent man, it was taking Spencer longer than it should to put this together. It showed that the idea of being with the blond man was so far from Spencer's mind he couldn't even process it, which eased

Emilio's concern. And watching him fumble and stammer was sweet. Emilio held his arms open in invitation, and Spencer walked right up to him, stood between his spread knees, and looked down.

"I'm twenty-two," he said when he realized Spencer wasn't going to form the connection on his own.

"That's different," Spencer said insistently. "You're..." He stopped talking and blushed.

"How's it different, *cariño*?" Emilio asked as he pulled Spencer down onto his lap.

"I don't know." Spencer shrugged. "Abe is a kid, still making his way. That's why he was here. He had a blowout with his family over coming out and wanted career advice. You're confident and mature. You know what you want and you go after it." As if realizing what he'd said, Spencer started stammering. "I mean, uh—"

"You mean like how I went after you?" Emilio asked, feeling good that his approach to get Spencer's attention had been spot-on.

Not answering the question, Spencer dipped his chin and played with the hem of Emilio's bright-orange company shirt. It was ugly as hell, but it stood out when they had jobs near traffic. Plus, with as dirty as his clothes got when he crawled through tight spaces checking on wiring, it made sense to wear something cheap and easy to replace.

"Anyway, you have no reason to be jealous," Spencer said.

"Sure I do," Emilio replied. "You're good-looking, nice, smart. Hell, I spent the past two weeks on this job site, hoping to get your attention." He put his fingers under Spencer's chin and lifted it. "And now that I got it, I ain't gonna let some other guy get in my way."

Spencer draped his arms around Emilio's neck and huddled closer to him. "You're the only one who thinks I'm some sort of catch," he said softly, sounding bashful but also pleased.

"No way. I bet you get propositioned all the time. You probably just don't realize it."

"It's nice that you think so," Spencer said, clearly not believing that to be true. Emilio felt sad that Spencer couldn't see his own appeal, but at the same time, he found that modesty charming. He brushed his hand through Spencer's soft brown locks and leaned forward to take a kiss. "You never told me what you were doing here," Spencer mumbled and then licked his lips.

The reminder was like being doused with a bucket of cold water. "Shit," Emilio said. "I was gonna pop in and say hello. We're down a truck, so my brother Raul caught a ride in today. I came by to pick him up and take him to a job we're doing in Spring Valley. I couldn't be so close without saying hi to you, but I promised him I'd only be a minute. He's probably gonna give me hell if I don't get back there."

Spencer hopped off his lap, and Emilio immediately missed his weight. With a disappointed sigh, he climbed to his feet.

"You look like someone shaved your cat," Spencer said with a chuckle.

"Shaved my cat?" Emilio opened his eyes wide in horror. "What the hell is that supposed to mean? Who shaves cats?"

"Nobody. That's the point of the saying."

"That is not a saying," Emilio insisted as he shook his head. "A saying is 'you look like someone kicked your puppy.'"

"Kicking puppies is better than shaving cats?" Spencer asked sarcastically, his eyes twinkling.

"Quit using your college logic on me, *Dr. D*," Emilio said, repeating the nickname he'd heard Spencer's student use.

Spencer shuddered and frowned. "I don't want you to call me that," he said.

Emilio laughed in response to Spencer's expression. Knowing he had such a strong negative reaction to sleeping with his students was comforting. Emilio hadn't given the idea much thought until he'd walked in on the handsome man in Spencer's arms and realized Spencer was probably surrounded by cute guys all day long. Not having to compete with them was a relief.

"So no professor-student sex games, then?" Emilio asked.

Looking truly horrified, Spencer said, "God, no. Let's stick to sexy electrician."

"How about you stick to *working* electrician, *hermanito*?"

At the sound of his brother's voice, Emilio spun around. Raul was holding the office door open and leaning inside.

"Hey, man, how about knocking?"

"Nah, what fun is that? This way I get some ammo on you." He pushed the door open. "Ain't you gonna introduce me to your, uh, friend there?"

Friend, right. Like anybody in the room believed that. Emilio rolled his eyes and said, "If you wanted to meet him, you could've asked, man."

"Yeah, right." Raul walked in, and Spencer, who was standing behind Emilio and slightly off to the side, scooted closer. "Henry already told me you said we had to wait." Looking around Emilio, Raul held his hand out. "I'm Raul Sanchez, Emilio's oldest brother."

Spencer cleared his throat, an obviously nervous gesture, and then moved forward so he was standing next to Emilio. "Spencer Derdinger," he said as he took Raul's hand and shook it. "It's nice to meet you. Emilio talks a lot about his family."

"A lot, huh? I doubt that, but I'm glad to hear there was at least some talking taking place this weekend."

Spencer turned beet red and Emilio growled. "Fuck you, Ro. Lay off."

"Oh ho, look at that. Little brother's getting protective of his man. I guess it's as serious as Henry said."

Even though he loved his brothers, they knew how to push Emilio's buttons like nobody else, making him revert back to childhood roles and reactions. Raul's words and tone were designed to piss Emilio off, and they worked exactly as intended. He planted both hands on his brother's chest and shoved him backward. They slammed against the wall and tussled for a few seconds, neither one of them coming out on top, then Raul reached underneath his arm and started tickling.

"Cut it out!" Emilio yelled and tried to wriggle free. "Seriously, Ro!" He laughed, breathlessly. "Stop!"

With his own deep chuckles filling the room, Raul finally relented and stopped tickling him. Instead he threw his arm over Emilio's shoulders and squeezed him fondly.

"Asshole," Emilio said as he threw him an elbow.

Raul smacked a loud kiss on his cheek. He shook his head and walked back over to Spencer to say goodbye.

"Uh, are you..." Spencer looked completely out of sorts as he shifted his gaze between Emilio and Raul. "Ahem. Is everything okay?

"Sure. Raul's being a dick." He looked back at his brother over his shoulder. "Ain't that right, Ro?"

"I don't know, *hermanito*." Raul shrugged. "Dick's more your area. I was thinking you were being a pussy."

Emilio threw his middle finger up and kissed Spencer's cheek. "Ignore him," he said. "He thinks he's a comedian."

"Are you sure everything is okay?" Spencer whispered, sounding deadly serious.

"Yeah." He pulled Spencer into a hug. "We were just foolin' around. You know how it is. You have a brother."

"I guess I don't. Steve and I haven't ever been, uh, close."

Emilio's heart ached in sympathy. His brothers could be a pain in the ass, as Raul had just proven, but Emilio didn't want to imagine his life without them, and he wouldn't change their relationship for anything. Before he could respond to Spencer, Raul was suddenly right there, squeezing Emilio's shoulder with one hand and Spencer's with the other.

Emilio realized Raul had overheard Spencer talking about his brother when he said, "Don't worry, Spencer. We'll make sure you're used to us before we start wrestling with you."

It was as close to saying "welcome to the family" as anyone in the Sanchez clan would get. Emilio covered Raul's hand with his own and patted him in a silent thank-you.

"I'll see you tonight, *cariño*," he said to Spencer. Then he leaned down and kissed Spencer one more time before following his brother out the door.

# CHAPTER 10

THOUGH IT was completely out of character, after only three weeks, Spencer was already used to his new routine. He'd wake up during what he previously considered the middle of the night and either kiss Emilio goodbye or, if he could manage to stay conscious after the first couple of kisses, they'd rub and touch and suck their way to sweaty, sticky fun. Then he'd fall back asleep for a few hours, go to work, and come home to find Emilio, often half-undressed, working on the remodel. They'd chat for a couple of minutes, after which Emilio would keep working while Spencer made dinner. The scent of food tended to make Emilio stop whatever he was doing and hit the shower, often dragging Spencer with him. After getting clean, they'd eat, snuggle on the couch as planned—with Emilio watching television and Spencer reading—and then go to bed. Sleep came an hour or so after that, with Emilio playing Spencer's body like a fiddle in the interim.

On Friday evening, Spencer pulled into his driveway and practically dashed out of the car, excited to see the progress Emilio had made on the house that day and even more excited to see Emilio.

"Emilio?" Spencer called out when he walked in the door.

When he didn't hear a response, he started searching the house. He had checked the living room and kitchen and was walking down the hallway to the bathroom when he heard a rustling sound. It took him a few seconds to place that it was coming from overhead and a few more to realize that meant Emilio was in the attic. With a smile, he set his briefcase down in the office-slash-guest room and then strolled over to the bedroom he now shared with Emilio.

Just thinking about Emilio made him happy. Walking in and seeing Emilio's boots in the corner, his wallet and cell phone on the dresser, and one of his many orange work shirts peeking out of the hamper, had Spencer practically glowing. All the great sex didn't hurt in the glowy-happiness department either. Never had Spencer experienced so many orgasms in such a short period of time. And these weren't solo jobs, either. Nope, every ounce of pleasure was wrung from him by a beautiful, kind, sexy-as-sin man. And though he still worried his body would stop cooperating, up to that point, all systems had been raring to go.

"Spencer? Spence, you home?" Emilio's deep voice boomed out along with heavy footsteps.

"In here," Spencer responded.

"Hey." Emilio smiled broadly as he walked into the bedroom. "How was your day?"

He kissed Spencer's cheek, and Spencer was struck by

the *normalness* of it all, the feeling of simple domesticity in a situation that was in no way normal or simple. Nobody set up house after knowing someone for a day. It was impetuous and crazy and—

"It's right for us. What anybody else does don't matter," Emilio said, making Spencer realize he had been thinking out loud. Then Emilio chewed on his bottom lip and furrowed his brow. "It is right for *us*, right? I mean, I know *I* like being with you and staying here, but if you don't—"

His need to assure Emilio that his feelings were returned outweighed whatever concerns Spencer had about how fast they were moving, so he quickly said, "I like it too."

Relief washed over Emilio's face. "Yeah?" He gathered Spencer in his arms and gazed down at him. "Good."

Spencer linked his fingers behind Emilio's neck and tugged him down for a kiss. It was getting easier, more comfortable to ask for Emilio's touch. "How was your day?" he asked.

After taking another kiss and nibbling on Spencer's lower lip, Emilio said, "It was good. The monsoon rained us out of the courthouse job in Henderson, so I was able to spend a lot of time here. I finished running all the wires and dropping them to the outlets and light switches."

"That's great. Are you all done for the day?"

"Almost. I need another thirty minutes." He slid his hand down the back of Spencer's pants and massaged his ass as he unfastened the top few buttons of Spencer's short-sleeved button-down shirt and pushed it to the side, making room for his mouth to work up yet another mark.

One of Emilio's favorite activities in bed was using his mouth on every part of Spencer's skin, often making deep, dark hickeys. Thankfully, Emilio was always careful to leave the evidence in areas that would be covered by Spencer's shirts. Given how much he enjoyed the strong suction of Emilio's mouth and the visual proof of the man's dominion over his body, Spencer doubted he would have the mental power to stop Emilio when they were in the heat of the moment.

As Emilio nuzzled his shoulder, he moved his long fingers into Spencer's crease and skimmed them over his pucker. Spencer bucked and moaned.

"Ah, damn, *cariño*," Emilio whispered huskily. "Want you so bad."

Spencer knew exactly what Emilio wanted; his man wasn't subtle. Over the past few days, whenever they had fooled around, Emilio had played with Spencer's ass. As much as Spencer wanted to feel the thick, hot shaft insistently pressing against his hip slide into his body, whenever they got close to penetration, Spencer started feeling panicked, which made his dick lose interest. The last thing he wanted was to disappoint Emilio by being unable to perform, so he diverted the encounters, often by sucking Emilio's dick down his throat.

Kissing and touching Emilio was heaven, and Spencer

was lost in that pleasure when he made contact with the bedroom wall. "Wha...?" he asked in a daze. They had been standing in the middle of the room and Spencer hadn't realized Emilio was moving them. He was looking at the wall behind him, his body twisted, when Emilio turned him the rest of the way around and ground his dick against Spencer's ass.

Reacting on instinct, Spencer's entire body stiffened. He reminded himself that he was with Emilio and that he wanted exactly what he was being offered. But his tense body ignored the pep talk.

"I better go clean up out there before I forget," Emilio said. He kissed Spencer's neck and stepped back. Whether he had noticed Spencer's panic or whether he hadn't intended to take things further at that moment, Spencer didn't know. "You got anything planned for us tonight?" Emilio asked. "'Cause if you don't, I thought we could go out."

"What do you mean?" Spencer was more than a little nervous at the prospect of spending the evening in a crowded bar filled with drunk men. "Like, out to the clubs, out?"

"Clubs? Nah. I only go clubbing when I'm looking to pick someone up, and I'm done with that now. I was thinking we could go out to dinner with my sister and her husband. They have a sitter tonight. You'll love Alicia. And her husband, Jim, is a really good guy."

"Oh." Spencer sighed in relief. Dinner at a restaurant with another couple he could do. "That sounds good."

"Cool." Emilio kissed his temple and reached for his phone as he walked out of the room. "I'll let Alicia know we can join them. She's been bugging me about meeting you all week, so she'll be psyched."

It was only after Emilio left the room that realization sank into Spencer. He was going to meet Emilio's family. Well, not the whole family. But still, he was going to meet Emilio's older sister and his brother-in-law, which counted as meeting the family. He had already met Raul, Emilio's brother, who had been a handful but seemed like a good guy. He had shown no indication of disapproval toward Spencer, but one person wasn't always a good indicator of the entire family.

What if Alicia had an issue with Emilio being gay but hadn't said anything because he hadn't ever brought a boyfriend home? Even if that wasn't a concern, what would she think about their age gap? Would she worry that he was corrupting Emilio? Where did the brother-in-law stand on all this?

Just when Spencer was about to work himself into a full-scale panic, his phone rang. Grateful for the distraction, he answered it without looking at the incoming number.

"Hello."

"Hey, babe." Hearing his ex-boyfriend's voice took Spencer completely off guard. He hadn't spoken with Peter in over a year, not since Peter had cheated and then ended their relationship. "What're you doing tonight? I thought we could meet at Windsor. Say, eight o'clock?"

Spencer moved the phone from his ear and looked at it, needing to confirm that he was in fact talking to the man who'd said he was boring, predictable, bad in bed, and probably some other things Spencer had managed to block out in the intervening months. Why he hadn't ended things with Peter long before Peter broke up with him was now a mystery. Once he made a visual confirmation of Peter's number on the screen, he decided Peter must have called him by accident. A misdial was the only thing that made sense.

"Uh, Peter." He cleared his throat. "This is Spencer."

"I know that. I called you, remember?" Peter laughed, the sound harsh and cruel. "Some things never change. You're still as clueless as ever. But that's okay. I can deal with it, which is what I want to talk to you about, actually. So I'll see you at eight."

Before Spencer could process what Peter was saying and respond, the line went dead. The last thing he needed was to hear more about all of his shortcomings and failings. He'd put up with way too much of that already. And besides, he had seen Emilio's reaction to him comforting a student, so he knew the new man in his life wouldn't appreciate having him cancel their plans to go spend time with his ex. Just thinking about Emilio being the man in his life made Spencer feel stronger, safer.

He dialed Peter right back. He would say that he couldn't meet him that night. No, he would say that he *wouldn't* meet him period. Not that night and not any other. End of discussion. Just when he had worked up a good head of steam, Peter's phone went to voice mail. Nobody liked listening to messages, to the point where it seemed people would do almost anything to clear the voice mail icon from their phones, anything except listen to the dreaded voice mails. Knowing a message likely would result in aggravation, Spencer decided to text Peter instead.

Without letting himself obsess about it, he typed, *I won't make it tonight,* and hit send. There, it was handled. With shaky hands, Spencer stripped out of his clothes and headed for the shower, hoping it'd help soothe his anxiety so he could give Emilio the fun night out he wanted.

"HEY," EMILIO said as he stepped into the bathroom, making sure to speak loudly enough to be heard over the rushing water. "You okay with company in there?"

"You, naked and wet?" Spencer pulled the curtain open and grinned, the expression seeming to take effort, which was strange. "Yes, I'm good with that."

Emilio flicked his eyes over Spencer's nude body and moaned appreciatively. He loved how Spencer was put together—firm but not bulky, a smattering of light-brown hair on his chest and trailing down to his pubic bush, a nice-sized dick, even in its flaccid state, balls that were a perfect mouthful, and that ass. He groaned again. He fucking loved Spencer's ass.

As he always did when they showered together, Spencer moved over to make room for Emilio under the water. "Thanks, Spence," he said. The smile he got that time seemed to come easier.

He reached for the soap and lathered up fast, then made quick work of washing his hair. Spencer stayed nearby the entire time, his big brown eyes taking everything in as he softly touched Emilio's hip, his shoulder, his chest. In response to Spencer's obvious admiration, Emilio's blood flowed south, filling his cock. Spencer always looked at him like he couldn't get enough, like Emilio was something special. It was a heady feeling and it made him hard, made him horny every damn time.

"I replaced the hot water heater yesterday," he said to Spencer, arousal making his voice sound thick and gravelly. "I put in a fifty gallon." Once he was rinsed clean, he crowded Spencer up against the wall. "That means the hot water won't run out."

Emilio slanted his mouth over Spencer's, lapping at his lips before tugging the lower one between his teeth. He shoved his knee between Spencer's legs and moved forward, nudging Spencer's balls with his muscular thigh as he slid his tongue into Spencer's mouth. Spencer rocked against him, moaning and kissing.

"Turn around, *cariño*," he said as he dropped to his

knees. He licked Spencer's testicles and looked up at him. In this position, he was sure to be nonthreatening. "Please turn around."

Spencer gulped, then nodded and turned so he faced the wall. He flattened his hands on the tile and whispered, "Like this?"

"Yeah." Emilio kissed Spencer's firm, pale ass. "Just like that." He gripped Spencer's hips and pulled him a couple of steps back while at the same time moving Spencer's legs farther apart.

After spending the past few weeks all over each other, Spencer knew what was coming next. He crossed his arms against the tile and rested his face on them, his entire body relaxing. "Love when you do this," he said softly.

Emilio spread Spencer's firm globes and got straight to work, licking his way up and down his channel. "Mmmmm," he said as he buried his face against the soft, hot skin. "I love doing this." He flicked his tongue back and forth over the wrinkled pucker, reveling in the delighted noises coming from his boyfriend.

Though he hadn't yet had the pleasure of sheathing his cock in Spencer's tight heat, he knew that day would come. Nobody could fake the kind of reaction Spencer had to any sort of anal play. He loved being touched, being kissed, being licked in that area. When Emilio wasn't careful, he found himself falling into a rage at the thought that some man had taken this from Spencer, had done something to make his sweet, brilliant boyfriend fear something he obviously adored.

He shook the nauseating thought off. Now was not the time to think about the past. No. It was an opportunity to remind Spencer of how good it felt to be touched by a man he could trust, a man who wanted only to make him soar with pleasure. So touch he did. He brushed his fingertips against the sensitive skin in Spencer's channel and penetrated Spencer's silky hole with his tongue, over and over again.

"'Milio," Spencer groaned as he pushed back against Emilio, the sound desperate, needy.

Emilio's cock throbbed, the head dark and leaking. With Spencer's scent and skin and sexy sounds swirling around him, he couldn't wait any longer.

"C'mere," he grunted as he grasped Spencer's waist and pulled him down.

Spencer followed his direction, crumpling to the shower floor and immediately turning to face him. Emilio sat on his ass and spread his legs, making room for Spencer between them. Without hesitation, he scooted close and circled his legs around Emilio's waist. Their cocks slotted side by side, and Emilio wrapped his big hand around them, the water easing the way as he jacked them with sure, firm strokes.

"Emilio!" Spencer's eyes were wide, his cheeks flushed. "Oh, God. Oh, God." He was the picture of arousal and so damn beautiful he made Emilio's heart hurt. "Ah!" Spencer yelled one last time as his head dropped. He bit Emilio's shoulder and clutched his biceps hard, digging his fingertips in as cum pumped out of his shaft and drizzled over Emilio's hand.

With the sound of Spencer in the throes of pleasure rattling in his head, it only took a few more strokes for Emilio to fall over the edge. He called out Spencer's name as he came hard enough to make the sides of his vision go black. They sat together, both of them gasping for air, Spencer nibbling on Emilio's neck and Emilio keeping a hold on Spencer's waist with one hand and his hip with the other.

"So," Emilio said. "What do you think of the new water heater?"

Spencer's shoulders shook. He lifted his head and looked at Emilio. "Best water heater ever."

"Right on," Emilio responded. "That means it was worth the ribbing I took from Martin."

Spencer snuggled back against Emilio's shoulder and started petting his chest. "Martin?"

"Yeah, my brother."

"I know. But what does he have to do with our water heater?"

His heart might have stopped at the "our" part of that sentence and how easily it flowed from Spencer's lips, but Emilio managed to keep it together before he drew attention to what Spencer's subconscious was already feeling.

"Martin was with me when I picked it up at the plumbing supply store, and he kept asking why two people in an eighteen hundred square foot house would need a fifty-gallon tank."

"Is that bigger than usual?" Spencer asked, each word

sounding drawn out and slow, something Emilio now knew happened when his boyfriend was deeply relaxed.

"Yeah, it is." He pulled Spencer closer and rubbed his back.

"What'd you say to him?"

"To Martin? Well, I told him to shut the fuck up. And when that didn't work, I told him we like to go at it in the shower and having the water run cold kills the mood."

"You did not!" Spencer's eyes were huge, his expression shocked.

"Sure I did." Emilio shrugged. "It's the truth and it got him to stop talking about the damn water heater. I may use that approach from now on whenever he rides me about anything."

Spencer chuckled. "Don't you think he'll figure out what you're doing? That doesn't seem like something you can keep up without him realizing you're trying to get him to change the topic."

"Don't matter if he figures it out. Nobody wants to hear about his younger brother's sex life. It might be worse than walking in on your parents doing the dirty."

"You're devious!" Spencer sounded a little more energetic now that the bone-melting aspect of his orgasm was wearing off.

"I'm the youngest of five," Emilio explained. "That's considered a key survival skill if you want to have any kind of privacy."

Spencer combed his fingers through Emilio's chest hair, the act surprisingly soothing. "My brother wasn't ever like that. He never asked what I was doing." After a pause, Spencer continued. "I don't know if that was because he didn't care or because he figured whatever was going on in my life wasn't interesting enough to know."

To Emilio, those sounded like the same thing, but he kept that opinion to himself because he couldn't see how it would do anything other than make Spencer feel worse. "You really don't have much in common with him, huh?"

"No. Steven has always been the life of the party. He can talk to anybody about sports. He has an endless list of funny anecdotes to share. Find a crowd, and he's usually at the center of it. I'm nothing like him."

"Thank fuck for that," Emilio said. Spencer furrowed his brow in confusion. "I'm sure your brother is fun at parties, but I'd much rather have you waiting for me at the end of each day than someone who needs everything to revolve around him. That shit would get real old real fast."

"I like knowing you're going to be there at the end of the day too," Spencer said shyly.

It wasn't new information. Every one of Spencer's emotions was telegraphed on his face, so it was impossible to miss his excitement whenever he saw Emilio. Even so, hearing the words was nice.

Emilio rested his forehead against Spencer's. "That means we're well matched," he said.

# CHAPTER 11

"DO YOU want to drive or should I?" Spencer asked as he dropped his wallet into the back pocket of his khaki pants.

"You got a preference?" Emilio responded.

It took almost a minute before his brain could process the question because Emilio was shirtless, clad only in well-fitting jeans and a thick leather belt. Spencer wanted to forget about the restaurant and eat *him* for dinner.

"Uh." Spencer licked his lips and dragged his gaze from the bulge in Emilio's pants up his rippled belly and well-defined pecs, and over to his face. "Uh-uh." He shook his head, both in response to the question and to clear away the lusty haze and stop sounding like an idiot.

"I don't like being a passenger," Emilio said. "It makes my stomach uneasy. But my truck is a pain in the ass to park, so how about we take your car but I drive?"

"Sounds good." Spencer's gaze dropped to Emilio's six-pack and then darted back up.

Emilio snickered. "Why do I get the feeling that you'd agree to anything if I ask when I'm almost naked?"

"Because you're a smart man."

Emilio threw back his head and laughed, making Spencer feel a little lighter, a little warmer. He was pretty sure what he'd said counted as flirting, which wasn't his strong suit, but based on Emilio's reaction, he figured he'd done all right. He smiled to himself as he pulled on a white polo shirt.

"Are you ready to go?" Emilio asked. He pushed his feet into a worn pair of Vans and flattened his hands over his black T-shirt.

Spencer admired him for a moment, yet again, and then sighed happily. "Yes. I just need to get my vest." He rummaged through his drawer and retrieved a gray argyle sweater vest. After he had it on, he made sure his shirt was tucked into his pants, his belt buckle was centered, and his vest was straight. "Ready," he said, looking up at Emilio.

Emilio was staring at him fondly, the sides of his mouth turned up a tad and his eyes twinkling.

"What?" he asked as he moved closer to that strong, tall body. Emilio drew him like a magnetic pull. He flattened his palms against Emilio's chest and tilted his head back. "What?" he asked again.

Emilio cupped his big palms over Spencer's ass and started kneading. "Nothing." He bent down and kissed Spencer's temple. "I think you're really cute is all."

"You keep saying that," Spencer pointed out. "I'm not sure you can describe someone who is old enough to be your father as cute."

He didn't mind having Emilio call him cute; in fact, he

liked it. But with a meet-the-family moment right around the corner and the unexpected call from his ex still wreaking havoc on his stomach, Spencer's nerves were getting the best of him. Sixteen years was a big age gap. Certainly big enough for Emilio's family to worry that Spencer was taking advantage of him. His internalized anxiety attack was disrupted by the sound of Emilio coughing up a lung.

"Are you okay?" Spencer asked.

"You are not old enough to be my father!"

"Sure I am." Spencer had no idea why he was insistently going down this path. It certainly couldn't lead anywhere good. He internally screamed at himself to stop but it was no use. "People have kids when they're sixteen all the time."

Something passed over Emilio's expression and he went from outraged to sad and then wicked. Before Spencer could process what was happening, he found himself being moved backward until he was pinned to the wall.

"Emilio?"

Emilio planted his hands on either side of Spencer's head and leaned close. "Do I look like a kid to you?"

His husky voice made Spencer tremble. Though he was younger, Emilio was taller, bigger, stronger, and rougher. Add to those physical attributes his confidence to the point of swagger, his patience, and his sensitivity, and there was no way to see Emilio as anything other than all man.

"No." Spencer gulped.

"That's good, *cariño*." Emilio rocked forward and pressed

his groin against Spencer, circling his hips so his hard shaft rubbed against Spencer's overheated body. "'Cause the things I wanna do to you are *real* grown-up."

Spencer whimpered and looked up at Emilio's handsome face in awe.

"You see that?" Emilio said, raising his hand to brush it through Spencer's hair. "You're cute as hell."

"Okay," Spencer said, his voice sounding weak and shaky. That little exchange had him achingly hard, and he then wanted to avoid the dinner out for a whole different reason—staying in meant getting naked with Emilio. He reached up and massaged his palms over Emilio's muscular chest.

"Oh, no," Emilio said with a chuckle. "You ain't gonna distract me. Well, at least not yet. We're meeting Alicia and Jim for dinner." He bent down and whispered into Spencer's ear, "After that you can distract me all you want." He nipped Spencer's earlobe, then backed off, winked, and said, "Let's go."

When Emilio had him all wound up, Spencer's focus tended to be on him, all the things they'd done together, and all the things he wanted to do. With all those thoughts overtaking his system, there wasn't room to fixate on anything else. So when Emilio said they were going, Spencer nodded, took his outstretched hand, and easily followed him to the car.

"Here you go," Emilio said, holding the passenger side

door open.

"Thanks." Spencer climbed into the seat and blinked up at him.

Of all the things he found beautiful about Emilio, his warm smile was at the top of the list. And right then, he received one of those smiles, complete with twinkling eyes, as Emilio bent down and kissed his cheek.

"Don't worry," he said. "You're gonna love Alicia and Jim."

That hadn't been Spencer's worry. He had actually been fretting about the inverse of that particular equation. But before he could ramp himself back into another internal frenzy, Emilio opened the driver's side door, climbed into the car, and blanketed Spencer's knee with his big hand, rubbing. Spencer covered Emilio's hand with his own and lolled his head to the side so he could watch Emilio.

Faster than he had anticipated, the car was rolling to a stop. "We're here," Emilio said as he pulled up to the curb. He jumped out and hustled over to Spencer's side of the car, opened his door, and reached his hand out.

Spencer blushed but took his hand without protest. "You're like an old-fashioned gentleman. I'm not sure what that makes me. Am I the damsel in distress?"

With a sharp tug, Spencer was once again yanked against Emilio's chest. "I'm not sure an old-fashioned gentleman wants to eat his boyfriend's ass for dinner. And you, *cariño*"— Emilio reached between them and squeezed Spencer's basket—"ain't no damsel. Plus, you've got your shit together. Being a little nervous about meeting my family is no biggie. Henry's girl is still real quiet when he brings her around."

"You have an amazing skill for calming me down, you know that?"

"Good. That means you'll have to keep me around."

Spencer wanted that, longed for it. He had convinced himself he was fine being single, which was partially true. He loved his work. Between his friends, the stack of books he kept replenishing, and the work he liked to do on his garden, his free time had always been filled. But having Emilio around made him realize that while he hadn't been bored, he had been lonely for a long time, probably long before Peter broke up with him and maybe even before he had moved to Vegas.

But it was different since Emilio waltzed into his life. Emilio's energy, his warmth, his strength, made Spencer's entire body feel alive, aware. Even when they weren't together, Spencer found himself remembering something Emilio had said or done. There was no way to feel lonely with Emilio's presence everywhere, cushioning Spencer's mind and heart.

With that thought in mind, Spencer took a deep breath, squeezed Emilio's hand, and said, "Let's go meet your sister and see if I can make a good enough impression to keep your brothers from taking you away from me."

"My brothers can't tell me what to do," Emilio growled, a hint of his youthfulness coming through in the defensive tone and scowl. "But it don't matter anyway, 'cause they'll love you too. My mama's already impressed that you went to school for so long and that you teach at the university. I showed her some of those papers you wrote, and she's real proud that we're together. I even heard her talking to her sister about you."

Spencer tripped. "You talked to your mother about me?"

"'Course I did," Emilio said, as if that should have been perfectly obvious. "I moved in with you. I couldn't do something like that without telling my family."

Stated that way, Spencer agreed that it made sense. Of course, he had yet to tell his own family about Emilio, but that was mostly because he hadn't talked with them since before they'd met. He thought about calling them, felt his stomach flip over from the idea, and decided to table it until later. His only priority right then was to get through dinner without doing anything to embarrass Emilio or make him change his mind about building something with Spencer that would last long after the remodeling was complete.

*"HERMANITO!"* ALICIA'S voice rang out through the crowd of people standing on the patio surrounding the restaurant. They were a mix of sophisticated professionals and youthful hipsters. It was the kind of place Jim's family frequented, and

Alicia had been married to him long enough to fit right in, but Emilio felt out of place, certain he made less money than everyone there, and that he had less education. He figured Spencer would be comfortable in that setting, though, so he threw back his shoulders and charged forward, keeping Spencer close.

"Hi, Alley Cat." He pulled his sister into a hug and kissed her cheek. "Hey, Jimmy," he said to his brother-in-law as he raised his hand. "How are you?" They shook hands and leaned forward for a sideways semi-hug. He looked over his shoulder and held his arm out, waiting for Spencer to take a couple of steps forward, then he rested his hand on the small of Spencer's back. "Spencer, this is my sister, Alicia Winters, and her husband Jim." He tipped his head toward his pretty, dark-haired sister and her slightly round, gregarious husband. "And this"—he beamed as he looked at the intelligent, successful man by his side—"is Spencer Derdinger."

He saw Spencer's eyes widen and then he gulped, but those were the only outward signs of the nervousness he had shown earlier.

"It's great to finally meet you," Spencer said as he shook first Alicia's hand and then Jim's. "Emilio has a lot of wonderful things to say about both of you."

"The way my brother talks about you, I half expected a halo over your head and harps playing in the background." Alicia grinned at Spencer. "Either that or a gold lamé thong and nothing else."

"It's a good thing you were wrong, hon," Jim said. "Because they require a shirt and shoes to be seated and angel wings would never fit between these tables. Speaking of tables, ours is ready." He draped his arm over Alicia's shoulders and nudged his chin toward the door into the restaurant. "Shall we?"

"So what do you think?" Emilio asked Spencer as they followed Jim and Alicia through the loud restaurant. "They're nice, right?"

Spencer seemed a little startled but no longer panicked. "Yes. Very nice." He looked from side to side and then lowered his voice as he said, "But I can't believe your sister made that underwear comment."

"I know." He hunched down and spoke into Spencer's ear. "If I was gonna have fantasies about you in sexy underwear, I'd choose one of those fancy jocks that'd show your ass and leave your sweet hole exposed."

He caught Spencer as he tripped, the reaction predictable along with the flush climbing up his neck.

"Emilio!" Spencer hissed.

"Yeah?" Emilio wanted to pat himself on the back for managing to sound completely innocent.

"You can't... You shouldn't... You—" Spencer was sputtering and panting.

"Yeah?" he drawled.

Alicia and Jim had gotten ahead of them, and he could

see them taking their seats.

"Do you really want me to get underwear like that?" Spencer whispered, taking Emilio off guard.

He looked down at his boyfriend to gauge whether he was joking. "You'd do that?" he asked as he shifted from side to side, trying to make room in his briefs for his thickening dick.

"If you'd like it, yes." Spencer looked up at him, his eyes wide, running his tongue over his plump lips. "I think I'd do anything for you."

Jesus. There were things to work through, Emilio knew that. Spencer had been hurt and he didn't trust easily, he had grown up differently, so his idea of family wasn't the same as Emilio's, and they were in different income brackets and different age ranges. But when Spencer said things like that, when he gazed at Emilio like he was something amazing, none of those issues seemed important. Working through all that shit would be worth what they'd get in the end. And Emilio had never been afraid of hard work.

"Emilio, man, you're blocking people," Jim called out. "Come sit down."

"Coming," he answered Jim without moving his attention from Spencer. "We'll talk about this when we get home, okay?" he whispered to Spencer. "I ain't gonna forget."

Spencer bobbed his head and then they went to sit down for dinner.

They hadn't been seated long enough for Emilio to get

his menu open or for Spencer to unroll his napkin from the silverware when Jim threw out the first question of the night. "Spencer, I understand you're a teacher. Where do you teach?"

The silverware tumbled to the table and Spencer blushed as he placed it next to his plate in perfectly straight rows. He glanced up and said, "I'm a math professor at UNLV."

Jim's eyebrows shot up, and Emilio knew he was impressed. Yup, his man was crazy smart.

"Wow, that's intimidating. The hardest class I had in school was through the math department. Business statistics." Jim ran his hand over his mostly bald head. "It's a miracle I passed."

"Oh, don't let Jim fool you!" Alicia said as she looked fondly at her husband. "He has a knack for numbers. Jim's a CPA. In fact, that's how we met. I interned at his firm when I was in college." She paused and then peered at Spencer. Emilio put his menu down and set his hand on Spencer's knee, reminding him that he wasn't alone as he faced the upcoming inquisition. "How did you meet my brother?"

"He was working on the addition to the building where I work." Spencer draped his napkin over his lap and fiddled with it. "And I, uh, saw him there." He turned his head and looked at Emilio from underneath his lashes. "He was smiling."

"Uh-huh," Alicia said, her tone indicating that she wanted more information.

Emilio rolled his eyes. "Raul asked me to come look at the electrical box and give him some ideas of what we'd need to do with wiring. I saw Spencer walking into his office and decided I had to find a way to meet him, so I chased him down and asked him out. Now quit asking so many questions. I just caught him; I don't want you scaring him off."

Spencer relaxed and grinned, his dimples flashing. "She's fine," he assured Emilio.

"You see that, Alley Cat? Dimples." Emilio put his hand over his heart and sighed dramatically as he flung his head back. "He has dimples."

"Goofball," Spencer said, bumping his shoulder against Emilio's, the gesture friendly and familiar.

"Yes, I see," Alicia said with laughter in her voice. "Spencer, you have lovely dimples."

Emilio waggled his eyebrows at Spencer. "I knew you'd win her over," he whispered loud enough for his voice to carry to everyone at the table. "You're irresistible."

Spencer blushed but his lips were turned up. "Only to you," he mumbled.

"No way." Emilio darted his eyes toward Jim. "Am I right, Jimmy?"

"What's that?" Jim asked as he glanced up from the menu. He looked over his reading glasses at Emilio and Spencer. "Oh, yes. Irresistible." Then he turned to Alicia and said, "Should we share the harvest salad and the fish or do you want to get your own meal?"

"What are you getting?" Emilio asked Spencer.

Tearing his gaze away from Jim and Alicia, Spencer bent his head close to Emilio's and quietly said, "Your family is amazing."

"Yeah," Emilio responded automatically. Then he furrowed his brow and asked, "What do you mean?"

"They're really accepting. It doesn't matter to them that we're both guys. Your brother was like that when we met, and now your sister and her husband too." Spencer took a deep breath. "Your family is amazing."

Emilio shrugged. "Yeah. They're cool."

"No, really." Spencer curled his fingers over Emilio's forearm. "You have a great family. You're lucky."

"Ah, *cariño*," Emilio whispered when understanding finally dawned. He cupped Spencer's nape, bringing them closer together until their foreheads were almost connecting. "I'm sorry it ain't like that for you."

"It's okay," Spencer said.

"No." Emilio shook his head and rubbed his thumb over the side of Spencer's neck. "It ain't right. You deserve better than what you got."

At first it seemed like Spencer was going to brush off Emilio's comment, which would have been typical. But then he slammed his mouth shut, took in a deep breath, and said, "You're right. But that's not why I said anything. I don't want you to feel bad for me, I just want you to know that your family's something special, and I'm glad you're letting me get to know them."

"'Course," Emilio said hoarsely.

"I'm going to order the fondue for us to share," Jim said, finally setting his menu down. As usual, the man was completely oblivious to the conversation around him. He stretched his neck and looked around the room. "Where did the waiter go? I'm starving. Are you guys ready to order?"

"I'm gonna get the burger," Emilio said. "What about you, Spence?"

"I want the soup and salad with chick—" Spencer froze midword, his gaze locked on something across the room. It was hard to tell in the somewhat dark space, but it seemed like the color drained from Spencer's face. "Excuse me," he said weakly as he pushed his chair back. "I, uh, need to wash my hands."

"No problem," Emilio said, his forehead creased with worry. He tried to follow Spencer's gaze, but couldn't see anything out of place.

"We'll go ahead and order for you," Jim announced. He picked up the menu once again. "Maybe we should get the ceviche to share."

"Tha...thank you." Spencer gulped. "I'll be right back."

# CHAPTER 12

SPENCER RUSHED away from the table so he could catch Peter before he got close enough to embarrass him in front of Emilio and his family. When he caught sight of his ex waving from across the room and making his way toward him, he thought he was going to be sick.

"I tried calling you to say I was running late, but the call went straight to voice mail," Peter said as soon as Spencer was within earshot. "You should really answer your phone. Did you put our name in?"

"Put our name in?" Spencer repeated, trying to process Peter's sentence and understand what he meant.

"Yes. There's a line out the door. Don't tell me you didn't think of it." He rolled his eyes and started charging back to the hostess stand. "Of course you didn't." When Spencer didn't follow him, he paused and looked back. "Come on," he snapped.

Wanting to avoid any kind of scene, Spencer dashed after him. "Peter, let's uh, go over there." He tilted his head toward a corner near the bathrooms. It was semi-quiet and, most important, completely out of view from the table where

Emilio was sitting.

"Why?" Peter asked. "Oh! Did you already get a table?" He shook his head. "I guess being late saved me from having to wait around, huh?" He laughed, the sound harsh and grating.

Spencer flinched. How had he stayed in a relationship with this man? And why had he ever been sad that it ended? He took a calming breath and then hurried toward the bathroom area. Peter stayed close enough that Spencer could hear him walking, feel him breathing. It made his stomach hurt. Then it got worse. He reached the farthest corner of the restaurant and started turning around when he felt hot breath on his neck and strong hands on his shoulders.

"You look good, Spencer." He knew it was Peter. He recognized his voice, he had asked him to come over there to talk, and he knew that Peter wouldn't hurt him, at least not physically. But none of those things kept him from breaking out into a cold sweat. He flipped around and raised his hands.

"Give me some space, okay?" he asked, his voice sounding shaky to his own ears. "I don't like—"

"Yes, I'm well aware of your many limitations." Peter sounded annoyed. He always seemed annoyed. But he moved back, giving Spencer room to breathe. "Honestly, it's not like I was asking to fuck you right here in the restaurant. Actually, that's one of the things I wanted to talk to you about. I know you have all those hang-ups about sex, but I have a solution that'll work for both of us." Seeming to notice their location for the first time, Peter furrowed his brow in confusion and said, "Where's our table? Did you order drinks?"

Finally hidden from Emilio's family, Spencer breathed easier. "No. No table, no drinks. I told you I couldn't have dinner with you."

"No, you didn't."

For a moment, Spencer questioned himself, but then he shook off the doubt and reached for his phone as he said, "I sent you a text."

"Oh, that?" Peter waved Spencer off. "Come on. You know I don't like to play games, Spencer. And your hard-to-get routine is old."

"Hard to... Never mind. Look, Peter, I wasn't playing games. I tried to tell you I couldn't make it when you asked on the phone, but you hung up too fast so I sent a text. Sorry I wasn't clear enough. I'll, uh..." Spencer stopped himself from automatically saying he'd talk to Peter later because he had no interest in speaking with the man again, ever.

"Look, I know you think it's cute or something to get me wound up in bed and then make one of your excuses, but I would have thought you'd have learned your lesson by now." Peter made a long-suffering sigh. "Taking it further by trying to get me to chase you to have dinner isn't conducive to my giving you another chance."

"I don't want another chance." Spencer's heart was slamming against his chest. Did Peter seriously think he had been playing games the entire time they had been together? That he had been toying with him when he couldn't get hard, when he couldn't stop shaking if Peter wanted to top him? "I sent you a text. I said I couldn't make it."

"You're here, aren't you?" Peter barked. "So we both know you not only could make it, but you did make it."

Spencer raked his trembling fingers through his hair. The one night he wanted to make a good impression, and he was neck-deep in an argument with his ex. "I didn't remember this was where you wanted to meet, Peter. I was surprised when you called, and then everything happened really fast and I didn't focus on the restaurant."

"Right." Peter rolled his eyes. Again. "Then why are you here?"

"I'm here for dinner. And, actually, I need to go because the food is probably there and I don't want them to wait on me."

Peter squinted. "I saw you sitting with those people, but I thought you knew that man from work and you were saying hello." His face screwed up into a glare. "Who are they? I don't recognize them."

"Peter, I can't do this. I need to go." Spencer started walking away.

"Wait. Are you dating that guy?"

Spencer didn't answer. He kept walking and hoped he wouldn't shake apart.

"Whatever," Peter said, disgustedly. "It won't last. The minute he takes you to bed it'll be over."

Dear God. At the volume Peter was using, other people

could probably hear him. Spencer looked down, half hoping the floor would open and swallow him, but he forced himself to remain upright and keep walking.

"How long do you think he'll put up with your bullshit, Spencer? Eventually, everyone wants to get laid."

He turned the corner and collapsed against the wall, barely managing to keep his knees straight so he wouldn't fall to the ground. With as long as he had been gone from the table already, another minute couldn't hurt and he really needed to catch his breath and get his racing heart under control. On the other hand, if he stayed there much longer, Peter might walk by and see him. Then they'd start fighting all over again. Spencer wiped his clammy hands on his chinos, took in a deep breath, and tried to put the past five minutes out of his mind as he walked back to the table. Back to Emilio.

"There you are!" Emilio said as soon as he got to the table. He looked relieved, which made Spencer feel good, because it meant he cared, but guilty, because it meant he'd been worried. Emilio leaned close to him and whispered, "Is everything okay?"

"Yes, yes. I, uh, ran into someone I know. I'm sorry about that," Spencer apologized to everyone around the table.

"Don't worry about it, Spencer," Alicia said with a wave of her hand. "You didn't miss anything except Jim complaining about how long it's taking for the food to come and me grilling my brother about you."

Emilio stared at his sister and said, "What are you talking

about? You weren't even—"

"So, Spencer," Alicia interrupted. "Did you grow up here or are you a transplant? Maybe one of those Midwesterners looking to get away from the cold?"

"I, uh, neither, actually." The mundaneness of the topic eased the knot in Spencer's throat. He could do this. He could make small talk, have dinner, act normal. Not have an emotional breakdown in front of the man he wanted to impress and his family. "I'm from Orlando. So I didn't grow up in Vegas, but I'm plenty used to the heat."

"Oh! Orlando. What do people from Orlando call themselves? Like, you know how people from Vegas are Las Vegans? Is it Orlandoans? I bet you get a lot of snowbirds there too, right? We were actually in Orlando just last year! Jim had a conference for work so we decided to take the kids and make a vacation out of it. We spent a whole week at Disney World. Had a great time. Usually we go to Disneyland, which is great too, but Disney World is so much bigger. Oh, and Epcot... You've been to Epcot, right? Of course you have, what am I saying? Anyway, so one morning we went to..."

Alicia smiled and chatted, telling him about her family's visit to Florida, about the hotel they stayed in, about each of her children's favorite rides, about the princess costumes her daughter wore on the various days they spent at the park, about the character meals, and all sorts of other details Spencer found amusing but wouldn't remember. By the time their food arrived, he was chuckling about a story involving the It's a Small World ride breaking down, leaving the passengers stuck listening to the song on a loop, and the interaction with Peter was far enough from his mind that he actually managed to eat.

THE EVENING had started out normally enough. They were eating at a fancier place than Emilio was used to and Spencer was unusually worked up, even for him, but both of those things were because they were with Jim and Alicia. No big deal. And then somewhere between starting the get-to-know-you game and paying the check, they had made a sharp turn and veered straight into the Twilight Zone.

In his entire life, Emilio had never seen his sister talk that much. Sure, she was friendly and sometimes even chatty, but not nonstop gabby. He didn't even have a clue what she was saying half the time. And when she took a break to eat a bite of food, which wasn't frequent, she seemed to put Jim on the case, insisting he relate some story or another. At first he didn't seem to notice that his wife had gone off the rails because he was so focused on shoveling down his food, but by about halfway through the meal, when Jim's plate was empty, he started giving Alicia strange looks. The only person who didn't seem to notice anything out of the ordinary was Spencer, but that was only because he had never met Alicia so he had no point of reference.

"Should we get dessert?" Jim asked once their plates were cleared.

"There's a great ice cream place next door," Alicia said. "Let's go there."

"Sounds good. Let me just get the check," Jim said.

"Please let me," Spencer jumped in excitedly as he reached for his wallet. "It'd be my pleasure."

"Why don't we split it?" Alicia said as she hopped up from the table. "Emilio, let's go find an empty table next door while they figure out the bill." She had her purse over her shoulder and was marching away from the table before anybody could respond.

"What the fuck?" Emilio mouthed to Jim.

He shrugged and shook his head, looking after his wife wide-eyed.

"All right." Emilio sighed deeply. "I better go with her before she explodes or something. We'll see you guys in a minute." He gave Spencer's knee a squeeze and then jogged off to catch up with his sister.

"Alicia!" he called after her. "Yo, Alley, hold up."

She kept walking until she reached the patio and then she stopped and waited for Emilio. "Hurry," she said and waved her hand toward herself quickly.

"You're the one who ran away." He caught up to her and then said, "What's going on with you?"

"Let's go over to one of those tables," she said, pointing

at the metal tables outside the ice cream shop next door to the restaurant. She stretched her neck and tilted to the side, trying to see behind Emilio. "They're still at the table, right?"

"Are you stoned?" Emilio asked. "Is that what you were doing when you disappeared into the bathroom for so long?"

Alicia grasped Emilio's elbow and started tugging him toward the table. "I am not stoned! I have three children, for Christ's sake."

"I don't know what one thing has to do with the other, and it's the only explanation for why you were gone for so long and then started acting like an insane person on speed."

They reached the tables and Alicia sat down. Emilio took the chair next to her and she leaned forward.

"I didn't go to the bathroom to do drugs, *hermanito*, honestly." She shook her head like the suggestion was completely outrageous, which would have been true if she wasn't acting twenty-five different kinds of crazy. "I followed Spencer and eavesdropped on his conversation."

"What?" Emilio shouted.

"Shhh," she hissed and darted her face around. "Not so loud."

"You snuck after my boyfriend and listened in on his conversation?"

"Yes! Now, we don't have much time, so if you want to hear what happened, stop talking and listen."

"No. This is nuts. If Spencer wants—"

Alicia cut him off and said, "The guy he ran into was his

ex-boyfriend."

Emilio stopped talking.

"I figured that'd work." She smirked for a second and then seemed to remember they had time constraints. "The guy is a total douche."

"Douche? Really? Who says douche?"

"Do you want to hear this or not?" she snapped.

He wasn't sure, actually. He had as much curiosity as the next guy, so, yeah, he wanted to know about Spencer's ex, wanted to know what had his sister in a tizzy. But it seemed wrong to get the information that way.

"Anyway, so Peter, that's the ex-boyfriend's name, was being really nasty. I guess he thought Spencer was going to meet him here for dinner and—"

"Why would he think that?" Emilio barked. "They broke up months ago."

"I don't know. It's not important."

Emilio disagreed with that assessment. He found the idea of Spencer meeting any guy for dinner was important, let alone one he had dated. But he wanted to hear the rest of the story, so he didn't correct her.

"Anyway, Spencer said he told Peter he wouldn't meet him, and Peter accused him of playing hard to get." She paused and gulped. "And then Peter said Spencer used to do the same thing when they were dating, only..."

Suddenly, Alicia went from hyper to sad, her eyes filling with tears.

"Only what?" Emilio asked frantically. "What'd he say happened when they were dating?"

"He said—" She put her hand on Emilio's forearm. "He said Spencer wouldn't have sex with him. But, *hermanito*, listen to me. The way Spencer was acting when Peter got close to him, and the way Peter was talking about how things used to be between them... I think Spencer was scared."

Emilio's hackles went right up. "Scared? Why was he scared? Did that fucker do something to Spencer? Why didn't you come get me?"

"No, that's not what I meant." She shook her head. "That Peter guy wasn't nice, but I didn't get the impression he had hurt Spencer." Emilio relaxed and Alicia added, "But I'm pretty sure somebody did." It wasn't anything he didn't already suspect. "You don't look surprised," she said.

"That's because I'm not. Look, Alley, I don't feel right talking about this with you. I don't think he'd want anybody to know, but...I've noticed some things and...I'm not surprised, okay? Let's leave it at that."

She chewed on her bottom lip and looked at Emilio thoughtfully. "Yeah, I understand, but if he's been sexually assaulted and it's impacting his relationships... Just tell me this: Have you had sex with him?"

"There are lots of ways to have sex," Emilio said stubbornly.

"You know what I mean, *hermanito*."

"Weirdest fucking topic of conversation with you *ever*,"

Emilio grumbled.

"I'm trying to help. You know I—"

"I know." He sighed. "No, we haven't had sex the way you mean, and, yeah, I think it's because he's been hurt. But it don't matter. Like I said, there are different ways to have sex, and even if we never...you know, it's fine. I don't mind."

That was maybe a bit of an exaggeration. Emilio had wanted to get inside Spencer's ass since before they had exchanged their first hellos, and he'd be disappointed if it couldn't ever happen. But he could live with a little disappointment if it meant staying in Spencer's life. And it wasn't like he wasn't happy with how things were going in bed. Spencer was magic with his mouth, with his hands, with his body. Hell, sex with Spencer was already better than anything or anybody else, so even if Emilio never got to fuck him, he could deal.

"Aww, *hermanito*." Alicia squeezed his arm. "You're such a sweet boy."

"I'm not a boy! I'm twenty-two years old."

"I know." Alicia smiled fondly. "You're right. You're all grown up, but I'm still ten years older than you and I've experienced some things you haven't, so listen to me, yeah?"

Emilio grunted his assent.

"A person who has been hurt before, badly hurt, has a hard time trusting, so if another person wants to have a relationship with someone like that, he better be really sure about it, because if he's just playing around and the other person trusts him but then he gets bored or gives up he can really hurt that person. More than with people who haven't been hurt, you know?"

"I don't even know if that was English, Alley, but I ain't playing around, I ain't gonna get bored, and I ain't gonna hurt Spencer."

"Not on purpose but—"

"Not on purpose, not on accident, not ever. Look, I know you're my big sister, but I'm not a kid. I know he has a past, I get it, but he's the *one*, you know? He's the guy for me. If that means no...uh, you know, that's okay by me."

Alicia leaned back in her chair and sighed. "Okay, fine. I can see you really care about him, *hermanito*, and I get it. He's real special, smart, handsome, worldly. But before you decide to write off sex because it's okay with *you*, make sure it's okay with *him* too, yeah?"

Okay, now he was really confused. "What does that mean? You just said—"

"I said it sounded like he didn't want to have sex with that Peter douche. I said I think he's been hurt. I said having a history like that might mean he'd never be able to have sex. But I didn't say any of those things were what Spencer *wants*." She blinked rapidly. "Sometimes we want something so much, but then when it's right in front of us, our bodies betray us and make us push it away, you know?" A single tear escaped from her eye and rolled down her cheek. She moved the back of her right hand across it and wiped it away. "If you really care about him, *hermanito*, don't give up on him. Saying you'll stand by him either way is wonderful. But if there's a way for him to be whole again, if you can be strong enough to help him with that..." She swiped at the corners of both eyes and swallowed hard.

"I understand," Emilio said, reaching for her small hand and taking it between both of his.

She nodded and sniffled. "Okay, good."

"Thanks, Alley. I'm sorry to make you go through this."

"Don't apologize." She cleared her throat. "Seeing the way you are with him... You've grown into a good man, *hermanito*. A strong man. I'm real proud of you." She stood up and kissed Emilio's cheek. Then she straightened her skirt and said, "Let's go. Jim and Spencer are probably already in line for ice cream, wondering where we are."

Emilio climbed to his feet and wrapped his arm around his sister's waist. They walked to the entrance in silence and then he pulled the door open, holding it so Alicia could go in first.

"If Spencer ever needs to talk, you tell him I'll understand. You tell him..." She swallowed hard. "You tell him I've been there and I came out good on the other side, yeah?"

# CHAPTER 13

"HOW LONG were we at dinner?" Emilio asked as they drove home. "Two, three days?"

Spencer laughed. "Oh, come on. It wasn't that bad." He thought about it for a few seconds and added, "Actually, I had fun tonight."

Surprisingly, that was true. Despite Spencer's initial reservations about meeting Emilio's family, and the unforeseen Peter fiasco, dinner had been really nice. Jim seemed like a good, albeit quiet, guy. Alicia was very sweet and very talkative. Emilio had been attentive and wonderful and everything anybody could possibly want in a boyfriend.

With that thought at the front of his mind and heart, Spencer twisted his body sideways and looked at Emilio. "Thank you," he said.

"Why're you thanking me?" Emilio asked as he quickly jerked his gaze toward Spencer and then refocused on the road. "You paid for dinner. I should be thanking you." He cleared his throat and said, "Thank you."

Spencer snorted and grinned. "See? That's why I'm thanking you. It was a, uh, stressful night, but you made it fun anyway." Spencer sighed softly. "I don't know how you do that. It's like you're magic."

"No magic," Emilio said. "Just a regular guy."

He reached his hand out and Spencer took it, hanging onto it for the rest of the short drive home and thinking Emilio was the furthest thing possible from being just a regular guy. They pulled into the driveway and Emilio squeezed his hand before pulling away to take the keys out of the ignition.

"Alicia liked you a lot," Emilio said, twirling the keys on his finger as they walked to the door. "And I think you and Jim have a lot in common. But we'll have to wait until the next time we see them for you to figure out what all it is. I'll make sure to bring a gag for my sister."

"She wasn't that bad!" Spencer said.

Emilio raised his eyebrows in disbelief. "Uh-huh." He unlocked the door and they stepped into the house, locked up behind them, and turned off the porch lights before heading for the bedroom.

"Anyway, Jim and I talked when you two were in line for ice cream. Did you know he plays chess? He said they'd have us over for dinner so we could have a little match."

"No, I didn't realize that. Is that something you like to do?"

Spencer shrugged. "I used to. Haven't played in years, but I'm looking forward to giving it a go again." He paused and then said, "He's much older than your sister."

Emilio yanked his shirt off and tossed it into the laundry

basket. Then he sat on the bed and began taking off his shoes. "Yeah. Alicia is thirty-two and Jim's in his midforties, I think." He stood up and unbuttoned his jeans, hooked his thumbs in the waistband, and pushed them down along with his briefs, and then scooped everything up and put it away.

As he always did when faced with a nude Emilio, Spencer ran his gaze all over the bronze, muscular body and sighed in appreciation. "Your parents didn't care that she married someone so much older?" he asked.

"Nope." Emilio strutted over and lifted Spencer's sweater vest up over his head. "And they won't have an issue with your age either. Quit worryin', they'll love you."

It wasn't until Emilio was pushing his shirt off his shoulders and Spencer's pants and underwear were already at his ankles that he realized he wasn't hard. For the first time since he'd met Emilio, he was standing beside his naked body and his body wasn't reacting at all. Instinctively, Spencer moved his hands over his groin, covering himself. Damn it. He had hoped he had gotten over this. He was about to turn around and find pajama pants when Emilio rubbed his palms over his arms and down to his hands.

"What're you doing?" he asked.

"Nothing, I, uh, nothing," Spencer stammered. Lord. He sounded like a buffoon or a teenager, and because he was neither, he knew he'd have to answer the question honestly. He closed his eyes, took in a deep breath, and said, "It's not nothing, actually." He willed himself to drop his hands, to stop hiding, but he couldn't. "We should—" He gulped and opened his eyes, forcing himself to meet Emilio's gaze. "We should talk."

"Okay." Emilio curled his hands over Spencer's and caressed them. "Let's get in bed, *cariño*. I wanna hold you, been waiting to do that all night."

The man was so sweet. Spencer wanted to keep him, wanted it so much. He blinked back tears and followed Emilio to the bed, hoping the thumping of his heart was only loud in his own head. Emilio pushed back the comforter and crawled in, pulled Spencer in after him, and then covered them both with the blanket.

"C'mere," he said, lying flat on his back with his arms open wide.

Though he knew getting close to Emilio would prevent him from hiding his shame, Spencer couldn't stay away. He flew into Emilio's arms and sighed in pleasure when the big man wrapped him in his embrace.

"It's okay," Emilio whispered, rubbing his back. "Whatever it is, you can tell me."

He didn't have a choice. Erectile dysfunction wasn't exactly something you could hide from the man you were sleeping with. Spencer knew that all too well.

"You're hard," he whispered. Then he pushed his groin against Emilio's hip and said, "I'm not."

"Oh." Emilio sounded confused. He moved his arm and started reaching between their bodies. "You want me to—"

"No," Spencer said. "That won't work. It's me. Sometimes I can't..." He sighed. "It's me."

They sat in silence for several minutes, and Emilio held Spencer tightly, his big hands rubbing Spencer's back.

"It hasn't been a problem so far," Emilio finally said.

"I know, but before that, it was." Spencer took a few breaths and steeled his nerves. "This happens to me, Emilio. It has for a really long time, and I can't control it." He swallowed thickly. "I'm sorry," he said, his voice breaking on the last word.

"Shhhh, come on now. So you can't get it up one night. It's not a big deal."

"Yes, it is!" Spencer snapped his head up and looked into Emilio's eyes. "I hate this! I hate that we're naked in bed and you're beautiful and I want you but I can't do anything about it. I hate that when I'm at work, I can't stop fantasizing about being on my hands and knees with you moving deep inside me, but when we're together and you try, I push you away. I hate that I can't control it. It's my body. I should be able to control it!" He lowered his voice and said it again, "I hate this."

"Okay," Emilio said calmly.

"Okay?" Spencer sniffled and caught his breath after his outburst.

"I was wrong to say it wasn't a big deal. I understand what you're saying, so let's figure it out."

"Figure what out?" Spencer furrowed his brow in

confusion. "What is there to figure out? I'm not... My body doesn't... I don't work right."

Emilio chuckled and said, "Oh no, baby, there ain't nothing wrong with your body. You've been working just fine." He peered into Spencer's eyes. "Talk to me."

Before he could stop himself, Spencer said, "I saw Peter tonight. My ex-boyfriend. He was at the restaurant." Emilio tipped his chin, encouraging Spencer to continue. "He called me today, while you were finishing up the work on the house. I haven't talked to him since we broke up, and then out of nowhere, he calls, says he wants to have dinner, spouts out the place and time, and hangs up. I sent him a text to say no but then he showed up anyway and he said..."

He let the words trail off, not sure he should continue.

"What did he say, Spencer?" Emilio's voice was level, but Spencer could hear the anger bubbling underneath.

"He thought I was playing hard to get, thought I used to do it when we were together too. But I wasn't. I'm not." He stared at Emilio, willing him to believe he was telling the truth. "It's not a game. I want you, Emilio. I swear I want you more than I've wanted anything ever. The way you make me feel... God, I..."

Deciding there weren't words powerful enough to explain what he felt, Spencer started sliding down Emilio's body, heading for his thick dick.

"What're you doing?" Emilio asked. "Spencer? What're you doing?"

Spencer fisted the hot skin and lowered his head. "Just because I can't get off, doesn't mean you shouldn't. I can still make you feel good." He licked at Emilio's crown and then dropped his mouth down over it and sucked.

"Fuck!" Emilio bucked his hips. "Spence, no." His voice was choppy, breathless. "Spence, stop, baby, please stop."

The words filtered into Spencer's brain and suddenly he realized Emilio didn't want him. That was it. It was over. Emilio was the best thing that ever happened to him, and he had driven him away. With his heart in his throat and stomach ready to empty, Spencer jumped back and scurried toward the side of the bed.

THOUGH HE had no idea what had taken Spencer from telling him about something important in his past to jumping into a frantic blow job, Emilio knew that if they were going to deal with whatever Spencer was going through, he'd have to be strong enough to resist the temptation of Spencer's amazing mouth and get his man to keep talking.

"Where're you going?" he asked as he shot up and grabbed Spencer's waist, stopping him from getting out of bed.

"I'll leave you alone," Spencer said, his voice sounding shaky.

He pulled the smaller man into his arms and held him tightly, petting his hair and rubbing his back. "Like hell you will," he grumbled into Spencer's ear.

"But you said stop. You said—"

"Ah, Spencer." Emilio sighed and tried to think of how to approach his skittish boyfriend. "Look, I ain't smart like you, okay? So you gotta help me out here. I think we need to talk. Before we went out tonight, everything was in working order and now it's not. That can't be a coincidence, right?"

After a few seconds, Spencer relaxed, his body no longer tense and struggling to run away. He rested his cheek against Emilio's chest. "No, not a coincidence," he admitted. "Stress can be one of the factors for ED."

"Okay." Emilio let out a deep breath, relieved that he was getting things back on track. "You were already nervous about meeting my sister. Your ex called out of the blue and then showed up at the restaurant. You had a rough night, Spence. It happens. Don't be so hard on yourself. I bet everything will be back to normal in the morning."

"What if this is my normal?" Spencer whispered. "What if the past few weeks with you were a fluke and this is how I'm going to stay?"

Jesus Christ, as tough as Spencer was on himself, no wonder he was so stressed out.

"It ain't gonna be like that. We both know your body works just fine. Do you think maybe everything that happened tonight just has you all wound up in your head and that's why you can't get it up?"

"I don't know. Maybe."

Emilio slowly slid his hand between them and cupped Spencer's package, the skin warm and smooth and right in his hand.

Spencer quickly grasped his wrist. "Emilio, I can't—"

"You don't need to get hard, Spencer. I'm just touching you, okay? I like touching you."

"O-okay."

He kissed Spencer's temple and gently rolled his balls. "Keep talking to me."

"What should I say?"

"Anything," Emilio answered. "Everything." He leaned close and spoke quietly into Spencer's ear, "I care about you, Spencer. You ain't gonna scare me away. Talk to me, let me help."

When Spencer didn't respond right away, Emilio worried he had made a mistake by pushing too hard. But then Spencer said, "It's not just the stress from meeting your sister and running into Peter. I've had this problem before, sometimes for months." He swallowed hard. "Something happened to me when I was young, Emilio, and I...I haven't been the same since."

Though the thought of someone hurting Spencer made him sick and furious at the same time, Emilio knew they had to talk about whatever happened if they were going to find a way to get out from under it. So he whispered, "Will you tell me?"

"Are you sure you want—"

"I'm sure," Emilio answered, sounding much more confident than he felt. He put his hand on Spencer's hip and caressed him.

"I was about your age," Spencer started. "Done with college, starting my master's program. I had been away from home long enough that I felt safe to be myself. I'd started going out to the bars, meeting guys, having fun. Then I met this one guy, and it seemed like it could be more than just a good time. We started dating. I slept with him. It was good. I was happy."

As jealous as he had been when he had seen Spencer comforting his student or when Alicia had said Spencer's ex had asked him out, Emilio didn't feel a twinge of the green monster right then. Spencer's calm, even tone scared the hell out of him. He pulled his man close, not letting him forget that, whatever happened in his past, he was safe now.

"Then one day, I saw him on campus," Spencer continued. "He was with a girl. They were kissing. She was wearing a ring, a huge diamond engagement ring."

"Oh, damn. What a fucker!"

"Yes. He called me that night, asking to come over. I told him what I saw, told him it was over between us. And I refused to see him after that. But he wouldn't stop calling and saying he wanted to explain, that it wasn't like I thought, and then one night, I went out drinking with my friends and he was waiting for me when I got home. He begged me to let him in so he could explain. I figured he'd say his piece and then he'd finally leave me alone, so I agreed."

Spencer paused and tilted his chin up, making eye contact with Emilio for the first time during the conversation. "Are you sure you want to hear this?"

No, he wasn't, but he nodded anyway.

"He said his fiancée had nothing to do with us, that we could keep seeing each other, said he knew I liked having sex with him. I called him an asshole and told him to leave." Spencer took in a shaky breath. "He said he was going to remind me, going to show me that he was good for me. He... he was bigger and I was drunk and..."

Emilio rubbed circles on Spencer's back.

"After he was done, he went into my bedroom and went to sleep and the next morning when he was leaving, he kissed me goodbye. Like everything was normal, like he hadn't... I switched schools. Made me lose a semester, but it was worth it to make sure I wouldn't have to see him again."

"Did you tell anybody? Did you call the police?" Emilio asked.

"No. There was nobody to call. You already know how things are with my family. And what would I say to the police? We'd had sex dozens of times. I'd let him into my apartment. I was drunk." Spencer shook his head. "Nobody would have believed me, and even if they had, then what? A trial? Testifying? No. I wanted it to be over. So I left and figured that would be the end of it. He didn't know where I was. He'd get married and forget about me, and I'd move on, put the whole thing behind me."

Trying to think of what to say, Emilio kissed Spencer's forehead. "You did it, right? You finished school. You have a great job and a house and a life."

"I do, but when I'm with someone, every once in a while I think of that night and I freeze up. It happens a lot if I try to bottom, and even if it doesn't, it's never as good as it used to be." Spencer trembled. "I used to love it, the stretch, that full feeling, moving together." He sighed wistfully. "Loved it."

Emilio moved his hips away so Spencer wouldn't feel his suddenly throbbing erection. Damn, he was a bastard for getting aroused during that conversation, but he couldn't help his reaction to hearing Spencer talk about how much he enjoyed getting fucked.

"Spencer?"

"Yes?"

Hoping he was doing the right thing for both of them and not being selfish, Emilio said, "Do you want to try? Will you trust me to keep you safe and make you feel good?"

"I want to. But what if I can't?" Spencer asked, sounding petrified. "What if I won't get hard? What if I freak out when you try to... What if I'm not strong enough to ever get past this?"

With his heart breaking, Emilio kissed Spencer's ear, his jaw, his neck. "Aww, *cariño*," he said. "Don't you see how strong you are? I don't know anybody who wouldn't be scared if they went through what you did. But being scared don't mean you're not strong. Nobody was there to help you, but you took care of yourself, you kept your life on track, you made a success of yourself. I don't know anybody as strong as you, Spencer."

They lay in silence, their bodies wound together.

"It's late. Are you tired?" Emilio asked eventually.

"Yeah. Are you?"

"Uh-huh." Emilio held Spencer close and kissed his shoulder. "Let's go to sleep. Tomorrow's a new day, right? We'll figure this out."

"Okay." Emilio's eyes fluttered shut and he'd started drifting off to sleep when Spencer whispered, "Emilio?"

"Yeah?"

"I know we haven't been together very long and it might be too fast for me to say this, but..."

Emilio put his hand on Spencer's neck and rubbed his thumb back and forth in a slow, petting motion. He could feel Spencer's heart racing. "Tell me," he begged, his voice rough.

"I love you," Spencer said.

"I love you too, *cariño*." Emilio smiled and buried his face in his boyfriend's neck. "I love you too."

# CHAPTER 14

USUALLY SPENCER woke up slowly. He'd float in and out of consciousness for a while, and even when he finally crawled out of bed, he was groggy until his second cup of coffee. But Saturday morning he awoke in a flash—deep sleep one second and wide-awake the next. Every minute from the previous evening was front and center in his mind, but after a good night's sleep, things felt less dreary, more hopeful.

It was Saturday, which meant Emilio didn't have work. Spencer sat up, tilted his ear toward the door, stayed perfectly still, and listened. He heard sounds coming from the other end of the house, proving Emilio was home. With that piece of information confirmed, Spencer relaxed despite all the memories bouncing around in his head. Being fresh on the outside often made him feel cleaner inside, so he figured a shower would help get the day off to a good start. Yawning, he stretched his arms up over his head, and then climbed out of bed and headed for the bathroom.

Fifteen minutes later, Spencer was awake, clean, and dressed in his most comfortable jeans, softest T-shirt, and a pair of slipper socks he got at a math department holiday gift exchange. He padded down the hall and heard Emilio talking, the words becoming decipherable as he got closer to the kitchen.

"That's what I did, Ma," Emilio grumbled. He paused. "No, that was the last batch. This one has eggs." Another pause. "I don't know. It don't look right."

Spencer walked in and saw Emilio holding his phone to his ear with one hand and a dripping spoon with the other while he stared into a bowl. He was shirtless and shoeless, wearing just his briefs and looking better in them than any model.

"Uh, kind of runny but with chunks too," Emilio said into the phone, and then he paused, furrowed his brow, and pursed his lips, looking ten different kinds of frustrated. "I did stir it, Ma!"

Spencer snorted out a laugh, the whole scene striking him as funny—a sexy man, barely dressed, whining to his mother while trying, and apparently failing, to cook something. As soon as Spencer made a sound, Emilio jerked his gaze away from the bowl and over to him.

"Shit!" Emilio said, followed shortly by, "Ma, I gotta go." He paused for a second and then whispered, "He's awake. I'll call you later." He moved the phone away from his ear, said, "Love you too," in a rush, and then he hung up.

They stood, staring at each other for a couple of seconds, and then Emilio said, "Hey. How'd you sleep?"

At the exact moment, Spencer said, "What're you trying

to make?"

"Fuck." Emilio dropped the spoon into the bowl, set the phone on the counter, and rubbed his palms over his eyes.

He looked so upset that Spencer hurried over to him and said, "What's wrong?"

With a sigh, Emilio lowered his hands. "I suck. I wanted to make you breakfast in bed, so I called my mom for help, but even with her on the phone, I can't seem to make pancakes."

Nobody had ever made him breakfast in bed. Well, technically that was still true because Emilio was having some trouble in the kitchen, but he was trying, which was just as great as getting the meal. Spencer's heart felt like it was swelling.

"I can make pancakes," he said as he walked up to Emilio and circled his arms around his waist.

"I know. You can make everything." Emilio cupped Spencer's ass and kissed the top of his head. "You're, like, a professional chef or something. But you had a bad night and I wanted to take care of you."

"You did," Spencer said.

"I meant this morning. I wanted to get your day off to a good start."

Spencer blinked up at Emilio and caressed his cheek. "You did," he assured him quietly.

They were pressed together, with Emilio wearing almost nothing, and though Spencer was feeling a little activity down south, it wasn't anything to write home about.

As if he could read Spencer's mind, Emilio said, "It's okay. Let's get some food in our bellies and then we'll go back to bed and figure this out."

"Okay." Spencer leaned over, looked into the bowl, and scrunched his nose. "But you go sit down and let me do the cooking."

"No!" Emilio said incredulously. "I want to make breakfast for you. Go back to bed and I'll cook."

"The things you described as chunky?" Spencer asked meaningfully as he looked up from the bowl.

"Yeah?" Emilio darted his gaze to the bowl and then back to Spencer.

"Those are eggshells."

Emilio leaned over the counter and peered into the bowl. "They are?"

Spencer stood next to him and calmly said, "Uh-huh."

"Is that why it's orange?" Emilio asked as he stared at the concoction he'd created.

"No." Spencer gulped. "I have no idea why it's orange, and, frankly, I think it's better that we don't think about it too much." He swiped the bowl off the counter, walked over to the sink, and poured the whole mess down the garbage disposal in a flourish. "There! I've disposed of the evidence," he said.

Emilio chuckled. "Are you saying my cooking is a crime?"

"No. Absolutely not." Spencer shook his head vigorously. "I definitely did not *say* that."

"Uh-huh. I see how it is." He stalked over to Spencer and crowded him until Spencer was leaning back against the sink. "We can go out to breakfast," Emilio offered. "My treat."

"Going out means getting dressed," Spencer said as he dragged his gaze from Emilio's face down his bare chest to his swollen groin.

"That a problem?" Emilio asked huskily as he planted his palms on the counter on either side of Spencer.

"Uh-huh." Spencer perused that tight body again and licked his lips. "How about I make us some french toast?"

"But I thought pancakes were your favorite?"

"I think we could use a little pancake sabbatical." Spencer glanced at the bowl in the sink and then looked up at Emilio. "Just until we get past the TPSD."

"You mean PTSD?"

"Nope." Spencer shook his head and grinned. "Traumatic Pancake Stress Disorder. TPSD."

"Very clever." Emilio reached over and started tickling Spencer's waist, making him screech and wiggle. "You're a real laugh riot."

"Emilio!" Spencer shouted breathlessly as he tried to push Emilio's hands away. His laughs were turning into embarrassingly high-pitched giggles. "Emilio!"

"Yeah?" Emilio asked, showing no indication of stopping his tickle attack.

"Can't...cook...if...can't...breathe," he said through laughter and gasps.

"Oh, man, we can't have that." Emilio stopped tickling and pulled Spencer into a hug. "You already promised me french toast." He pressed his mouth to Spencer's neck and said, "I loooove french toast."

Being with Emilio was fun, so much fun. Spencer clung to him as he caught his breath. "I'm going to seek revenge for the tickle attack," he said, glaring at Emilio and trying to sound dangerous but ruining the effect with more giggles.

"Have I ever told you how much I like your laugh?" Emilio asked. "Seriously, you have the best laugh." He traced Spencer's lips with one finger. "And you already know how I feel about your dimples." He sighed dramatically.

Spencer's cheeks heated. He dipped his head. "You're not going to distract me from my revenge plot."

"I ain't trying to distract you, Spence. You go ahead and do the tickle-revenge thing. Something tells me I'm gonna like it."

"You are not supposed to enjoy it!" He snapped his head up. "That defeats the whole purpose."

Emilio arched his eyebrows and said, "Well, you're gonna have to pay attention to me for the whole revenge thing, right?" He shoved his groin against Spencer's, circled his hips, and leaned down to whisper in his ear. "I like having your attention, *cariño*."

Spencer's breath caught for a whole different reason. When Emilio thrust his thick cock against him again, he groaned and said, "You always have my attention." Spencer grasped Emilio's hips and rocked forward. "I think about you all the time."

"That's good." Emilio bent down and started nibbling on Spencer's neck, continuing the motion of his hips. "'Cause I haven't stopped thinking about you since that day I saw you walking by looking so damn cute I wanted to fucking eat you alive." He pushed forward, hard.

"Emilio!" Spencer gasped.

"Feel good?" Emilio nipped at his ear and then straightened his neck, meeting Spencer's gaze.

"Yes." Spencer's voice was shaky and hoarse.

"That's good, Spence." He dropped his hand between them and squeezed Spencer's dick. "It's real good."

He moaned and closed his eyes, enjoying the pressure of Emilio's big hand stroking his erection. And then it hit him. He snapped his eyes open and stared at the warm, chocolate eyes studying his face.

"Emilio?"

"Uh-huh." Emilio looked immensely pleased.

"I'm..." Spencer gulped and dropped his gaze to his groin.

"Yeah, I know." He skated his hand up Spencer's ridge and then reached for the button on his jeans. "You want me to take care of you right here?"

The thought made Spencer moan with need, but he shook his head. "No. I need to make breakfast, remember?"

"Breakfast can wait for a few minutes."

Spencer bit his bottom lip and looked up at Emilio from

underneath his lashes. "I want to stay like this for a little while," he confessed. "I wasn't sure when I'd be able to..." He shuddered and took a deep breath. "It feels good. I don't want it to end yet."

"I'm glad." Emilio kissed his cheek, gave him a quick hug, and then reached for the sponge. "I'll clean up while you cook."

With a nod, Spencer moved away, heading for the refrigerator to get the eggs and milk, his belly sore from all the laughing, a huge smile on his face, and his dick hard enough to pound nails. Emilio really was like magic.

WHEN HE was done with the dishes, Emilio hopped up on the counter and watched Spencer dip slices of bread into a shallow bowl filled with an egg mixture and then set the soggy bread on a sizzling frying pan.

"That looks gross," he said.

Spencer chuckled. "It'll taste good. We just need to be patient while it cooks through." After a couple of minutes, he picked up one piece with a set of tongs and flipped it over, revealing a golden-brown masterpiece. "See?"

"Mmm." Emilio's stomach growled. "Looks yummy."

"Get a plate and you can start eating while the rest fries."

"No," Emilio protested even as his stomach growled

again, seeming to disagree with him. "I can wait."

Spencer looked meaningfully at Emilio's stomach and then raised his gaze to lock with Emilio's.

"Okay, maybe just one piece," Emilio said. He slid off the counter, got two plates and two forks, and came back to Spencer. "You have to eat with me."

"I'm not that hungry," Spencer said as he put two pieces of french toast on Emilio's plate. "There's syrup in the fridge."

Emilio set the plates and silverware on the counter and then cupped Spencer's ass with one hand and his balls with the other, squeezing and massaging.

"Ungh!" Spencer cried out in surprise.

"I'll get the syrup." Emilio grinned wickedly and waggled his eyebrows as he walked away.

"You're incorrigible."

"Is that a complaint?" Emilio called back over his shoulder as he searched the fridge for syrup. He turned around to see Spencer shaking his head and blushing. "Yeah, that's what I thought," he said smugly.

The stress Spencer suffered about his perceived shortcomings in the bedroom was horrible, but one thing it seemed to do was make Spencer appreciate arousal in a way that was brand new for Emilio. Whether it was because he had always lived in crowded quarters or because he hadn't ever had a real boyfriend or because the guys he had dated hadn't been as mature as Spencer, Emilio didn't know. But for whatever reason, in his experience, sex had been something to be enjoyed immediately and quickly, with him and whatever partner he had at the time rushing to get off as fast as possible. Spencer, on the other hand, was happy to stay wanting, to get worked up and remain that way. And Emilio had to admit, he liked that—liked being hard, liked touching and playing, liked ramping them both up and keeping them there. It was hot as hell.

He hopped back onto the counter next to the stove and poured some syrup on his plate. "Smells great," he said as he tore a piece of french toast off, dipped it into the syrup, and then popped it in his mouth. "Oh, wow." Emilio chewed and swallowed fast, immediately reaching for another piece. "This is so good." He chewed and moaned, getting lost in the enjoyment of the food. "Where'd it go?" he asked when he came up empty reaching for the next bite. He darted his gaze around the room.

"In your stomach!" Spencer said with a laugh. "Where do you think it went?"

"I didn't eat two slices of french toast." Emilio licked his lips. "Did I?"

With another laugh, Spencer picked two more slices of bread off the skillet and slid them onto Emilio's plate.

"Thanks!" Emilio stuffed a huge piece into his mouth. "There gonna be enough left for you?"

"Yes. Don't worry about me. Eat." Spencer looked at him and smiled, flashing his dimples. "I love how exuberant you are about everything."

Emilio furrowed his brow, but kept eating as he repeated Spencer's word, "Exuberant?"

"Excited. Like now." Spencer nudged his chin toward Emilio's already almost empty plate. "I make french toast and you make me feel like it's a gourmet meal."

"I don't know nothing about gourmet food." Emilio popped another piece of bread into his mouth and kept talking while he chewed. "But, man, you are incredible in the kitchen." He swallowed and then licked his lips. "This is the best breakfast I've ever had." He paused. "Well, that omelet you made last week was really good too, so maybe it's a tie." He furrowed his brow in thought and then added, "Oh, and that oven pancake thing with the apples and the lemons?" Emilio groaned and closed his eyes, a look of utter bliss on his face. "Seriously, man, the best." He picked up the last piece, swiped it through the syrup, and held it up to Spencer's mouth. "Open."

Spencer parted his lips and Emilio fed him the sweetened bread.

"Good, right?" Emilio asked.

Spencer nodded and darted his tongue out to lick some errant syrup.

In a heartbeat, Emilio was off the counter. "Let me," he said before leaning down and running his tongue over Spencer's lips.

There was a moan and Emilio wasn't sure whether it was his or Spencer's.

"You know," Emilio rasped as he swiped his tongue over Spencer's lip again, "some people use syrup and other food for sex."

Spencer scrunched his nose in distaste. "That sounds sticky and messy."

Emilio snorted. "Yeah, I guess it does." Suddenly, a flush crawled up Spencer's neck and he lowered his gaze. "What's wrong?" Emilio asked as he put two fingers under Spencer's chin and lifted it.

"Nothing. I know I'm boring." He gulped. "Sorry."

"Spence, you are the furthest thing from boring."

"I mean, in bed. I know I'm not really adventurous or whatever, but I can try." He stared at Emilio, looking a little desperate and making Emilio's chest ache. "If you want to, uh, use the syrup or do something else. I'll try."

"I'm not some wild guy, Spencer. I wake up at five in the morning, work hard all day, and all I'm looking for after that is a decent meal, good company, and someone to kiss and touch and"—he winked—"do some other stuff too, but nothing crazy. I ain't into all that shit." He gathered Spencer close to him and nuzzled his neck. "Besides, I like how you taste. Don't see the point in covering that up."

"Are you sure?" Spencer melted against him, draped his arms over Emilio's shoulders, and massaged the back of his head. "I know you said you wanted me to get that underwear. I can do that."

"Oh, fuck," Emilio groaned and cupped Spencer's

backside, squeezing and kneading. "Yeah, seeing your ass in a sexy jock would be hot. But I've never understood those guys that get dressed up in the leather clothes and hats and boots, or all the weird shit people buy on the Internet to wrap around their dicks or shove up their asses." Emilio shrugged. "I don't know how they can take it seriously, you know? Ain't sex enough for them? Why they gotta fuck with it?"

Spencer moved his hand to Emilio's cheek. "You are the perfect guy for me," he whispered and then immediately blushed.

Emilio turned his face and kissed Spencer's palm. "I like hearing you say things like that, *cariño*. Don't hide what you're feelin' because you think you're gonna scare me off. It ain't gonna happen."

"Okay." Spencer reached for the knob and turned off the burner, then rested his cheek against Emilio's shoulder and trailed his fingers over Emilio's chest. "Emilio?" he said after a couple of silent minutes.

"Uh-huh." Emilio kissed his head.

"Can we try to…" Spencer chewed on his bottom lip. "Can we go to bed and…"

Emilio knew what Spencer wanted, but he didn't have the right words for it either. There were too many feelings involved, too many ghosts they were trying to vanquish, too much emotion wrapped up between them to call it fucking. And sex sounded like something a doctor would say, something that didn't take into account everything it would mean to Spencer to join together that way and have it feel good and right. Hell, it was going to mean a lot to Emilio too.

"You wanna make love?" Emilio asked, finally settling on a term that sounded sort of hokey but seemed to fit.

Spencer relaxed and sighed happily. "Yes. Do you?"

"Oh, yeah." Emilio groaned. "In fact"—he grasped Spencer's shoulders and moved him back just enough so they could look each other in the face—"I got tested right after I moved in here, and I'm clean. If you don't want to, I understand, but I wanna do you bare." He rubbed his lips together. "Will you let me do you bare?"

Spencer whimpered and nodded, his heart racing, breath coming out in pants.

"Come on," Emilio said. "Let's go to bed." He slipped his hand around Spencer's and tugged him out of the kitchen, toward the bedroom.

"If I freak out—"

Emilio stopped in his tracks and turned on his heel so he was looking right into Spencer's eyes. "Spence, we don't have to do this. I want to. I want you so damn bad it makes my teeth hurt. And I know you want it too. But if it's too much right now, you'll tell me and we'll do something else. We can always try again tonight or tomorrow or next week or next month."

"You'll still be working on the remodel next month?" Spencer asked the question hoarsely, and Emilio understood that the words meant something else entirely.

"Probably," he said. "But that's got nothin' to do with it. I know I kinda strong-armed you into letting me move in here, but—"

"I could've found someone else to do the work once I had more money saved up," Spencer said. "I've waited almost four years—what's a couple more?" He took a deep breath and said, "I wouldn't have let you move into my house if I didn't want you here, Emilio."

Emilio cupped Spencer's cheek and caressed him gently. "I asked to move in because I wanted to build something with you, but it was never about remodeling your house," he explained.

"It wasn't?" Spencer asked, looking so hopeful that Emilio knew he'd happily put himself out there and share everything so Spencer would have no cause to doubt how he felt.

"No, *cariño*. I want to build a life with you."

A bright, dimpled smile was his reward. "I want that too," Spencer said. "And if we do it right, it'll take much longer than another month."

Emilio grinned. "Now you're getting it." He took Spencer's hand again and led him into the bedroom. "You know my parents have been married for thirty-five years," he said. "And they're still building."

Spencer squeezed his hand, and Emilio knew they were finally on the same page.

# CHAPTER 15

WITH HIS heart thumping so hard it felt like it was going to beat itself right out of his chest, Spencer followed Emilio into the bedroom. The hard-on he had enjoyed when he was cooking and playing in the kitchen had wilted in a fit of nerves. Whether Emilio noticed or not, Spencer didn't know, but he stayed right on task, stripping Spencer's clothes off as soon as they were in the room, then pushing down his own briefs.

He walked over to the nightstand, pulled out a bottle of lube and tossed it on the bed before coming back and playfully saying, "Hi," as he pressed his warm, hard body to Spencer's.

"Hi."

Emilio cupped Spencer's cheek, brushing his thumb over his lips. "Do you trust me?" he asked evenly.

"Yes," Spencer responded right away. "That's not why—"

"I know," Emilio said.

"Then why did you ask that?"

"Because I wanted to make sure you remembered." He bent down and brushed his lips over Spencer's. "Do you trust me?" he whispered.

This time Spencer thought about the question, absorbed it, made sure every part of him was in agreement when he said, "Yes."

"Good." Emilio nibbled his way across Spencer's jaw and over to his ear. "That's real good."

The tightness in Spencer's belly uncoiled, and he sought Emilio's mouth with his own. As soon as they connected, Emilio tangled his fingers in Spencer's hair and held him close while they shared kisses and licks. When Spencer was short of breath and weak-kneed, they tumbled to the bed, grinding against each other, and joined their mouths for more drugging kisses as they let their hands roam freely.

Sometime during all the touching and licking and nibbling, when he had stopped thinking about anything but Emilio's taste and scent and touch, Spencer got hard again. He moaned and reached for Emilio's hand, then placed it on his swollen shaft. "You do this to me," he said, his voice sounding gravelly. "Make me feel so much. Make me feel so good."

"Fuck, yeah," Emilio groaned in response to Spencer's confession. He dropped his mouth onto Spencer's neck and sucked hard as he fisted Spencer's dick.

"Gonna take care of you, *cariño*. Gonna remind you how good it can be."

With Emilio touching and sucking and stroking him, Spencer didn't realize they were moving until he was lying on his belly and Emilio was draped over his back. His first instinct was to panic, but then Emilio licked his ear and said, "Don't worry. Just my mouth first."

Before Spencer could process the words, Emilio's hot breath blew against his backside, followed by gentle kisses. He breathed out and relaxed.

"You have the best ass," Emilio rasped. He grasped Spencer's round globes and rubbed his thumbs along the channel before pulling them apart, leaving Spencer completely exposed.

It should have been embarrassing, but Emilio moaned and said, "So damn sexy. Wanna make a meal out of you," filling Spencer with so much arousal there wasn't room for anything else. Thick thumbs massaged Spencer's sensitive skin, increasingly focusing on his pucker, and then Emilio's morning stubble dragged against him, followed by his breath, and then finally Emilio pressed his lips over his hole and flicked his tongue back and forth.

"Emilio! Oh, God." He arched his back, raising his butt up as he spread his legs. "Love when you do that."

"I could do this forever," Emilio mumbled between licks. Then he slid his tongue across Spencer's opening and pressed his way inside.

Spencer's mouth opened in a soundless cry as he stretched his neck back and forgot to breathe.

"That's it," Emilio said when he pulled his tongue out and replaced it with both thumbs.

"Ungh!" Spencer moaned, no longer able to formulate

words.

Emilio moved his thumbs apart, spreading Spencer open and making room for his tongue to wander back inside.

After dropping his head to the mattress and tucking his knees underneath his body, Spencer stopped thinking entirely. He reveled in how good it felt to be penetrated by fingers and tongue and moved his hips back and forth, enjoying the in and out drag. Emilio stayed right with him, piercing his body with those digits over and over again, bringing Spencer right to the edge and keeping him there until Spencer was sure he'd die if he didn't get something more, something bigger.

"Emilio," Spencer gasped, the name sounding like a plea. "I need you."

"I'm right here, *cariño*." Emilio circled his arm around Spencer's waist and pulled him up until he was kneeling on the bed.

Even with his head fuzzy with arousal, he noticed that Emilio had situated them so they were sideways on the bed, with the open door directly in Spencer's line of sight. That wasn't an accident. *Do you trust me?* Spencer heard the question in his mind and knew the answer would never change, not with this man. Emilio wouldn't ever hurt him.

He looked back over his shoulder and watched Emilio reach for the bottle of lube. Emilio slicked his veined, thick shaft and rubbed it between Spencer's ass cheeks. Spencer moaned and dropped his chin to his chest as he closed his eyes, letting the wonderful feelings wash over him.

"Still good?" Emilio whispered in his ear, dragging his hard dick back and forth over Spencer's opening. "You said this was your favorite position, right? From behind?" He flattened one palm on Spencer's belly and massaged his pecs with the other.

"Yes." Spencer blinked away happy tears. He was no longer surprised by Emilio's sweetness, but he was touched that Emilio paid such close attention to everything he said. He reached behind himself and gripped Emilio's dick, then moved it until the mushroom head pressed against his rosebud. Then he held it in place as he pushed back, not stopping until the flared glans made its way past the tight ring of muscle and into his body.

"Ah, Jesus, Spence," Emilio groaned. "So tight."

Hearing Emilio's voice, shaky with need, ramped up Spencer's arousal. He had done that; he had made Emilio moan. He was the reason the thickly muscled body behind him was trembling. It was a powerful feeling, knowing he could give Emilio pleasure. He moved his right hand to Emilio's hip, holding on tightly. Then he looked back over his shoulder, lifted his left arm behind his head and cupped Emilio's neck.

With their gazes locked together and their breath mingling, Spencer pushed back while Emilio pressed forward, neither of them stopping until Emilio's balls were nestled against Spencer's backside.

"Love you," Emilio said into Spencer's mouth before kissing him gently. "Make me feel so good."

"Me too."

With his eyes locked on Spencer's, Emilio slowly dragged his dick out until just the glans was inside, then he thrust forward, burying himself back inside.

"Ungh," Spencer moaned. "Again."

"Yeah?"

Spencer nodded. "'S good." He reached for Emilio's hand and placed it over his groin. "I'm not scared," he said truthfully.

Emilio gave him a soft smile and kissed the side of his lips. Then he sat back on his heels and pulled Spencer down with him so he was sitting on Emilio's lap with that thick shaft buried deep inside.

"Together," Emilio said.

Spencer rested his head on Emilio's shoulder and bounced in counterpoint to Emilio, moving up when Emilio dropped down and pushing back when Emilio thrust up. The room filled with sounds of their bodies slapping together, Emilio sliding his hand over Spencer's shaft, and both of them grunting.

"God," Spencer moaned. "You fill me just right." He sped up his pace. "It's better than I remembered."

Emilio tweaked his nipples, fisted his dick, and pumped hard and deep into his body, faster and faster.

"Oh! Almost there," Spencer gasped in surprise. "Don't

want to stop. Never want to stop."

"We won't," Emilio promised him. "We can do this again whenever you want, *cariño*. For always."

Spencer looked into his eyes, still moving on and off his dick. "Promise?"

"Yeah," Emilio said, and then his eyes widened and he picked up the pace of his thrusts and tugged frantically on Spencer's dick. "Spence!"

"Oh God, I'm there." Spencer dropped down as hard as he could onto Emilio's lap and when Emilio's thumb rubbed over his crown, he screamed and came.

The first shot hit the base of his neck, the second his chest. He lost track after that, the pleasure so intense he forgot to breathe and the world went a little black around the edges. When he could finally focus again, he found himself lying on Emilio's chest, both of them stretched across the bed, Emilio peppering his cheek and neck with kisses.

Spencer wiggled around until he could connect his mouth with Emilio's and then he licked and nibbled on his lips. They stayed quiet save for a few moans and whimpers, exchanging kisses and touches, and Spencer realized it had never been like that. Not with any of his boyfriends, not even before he had been hurt. Not ever.

Emilio was special—that was something Spencer had known from the start. But it was more than that. Their connection was unique. With two decades of dating under his belt, Spencer understood that, understood he needed to cherish the relationship and hang on tight.

He lifted his face, gazed into Emilio's eyes, and said, "Thank you."

"I was just gonna say the same thing." Emilio brushed his fingers through Spencer's hair. "Thank you for trusting me, *cariño*."

"You make it easy."

Emilio beamed. "Good." He squeezed Spencer tightly. "Wanna take a nap?"

"Mmm hmm." Spencer found the blanket, shook it out, and then draped it over their bodies. He snuggled up to Emilio, his head on Emilio's broad shoulder, his hand on Emilio's muscular chest, and his leg draped over Emilio's hip. With a contented sigh, Spencer closed his eyes and fell into a peaceful sleep.

"WHERE'RE YOU going?" Spencer mumbled when Emilio started climbing out of bed Friday morning.

He turned around and kissed one of Spencer's closed eyelids. "Gotta go to work. Call me when you wake up."

"Mmm." Spencer reached out and grabbed Emilio's wrist. "Don't want you to go." He wiggled over to where Emilio was sitting and kissed his knee, then he dropped his hand onto Emilio's lap and went straight for his dick, trailing his fingers over it. "Do you have time to stay for a little longer?"

"Goddamn." Emilio shivered. Once Spencer's barriers had come down, he had been relentless. They had spent the entire weekend in bed, and Spencer had pounced on him the second he walked in the door every evening. "My dick's never had so much activity in such a short period of time."

"Is that a complaint?" Spencer asked as he started rubbing him. "Are you sore?" Spencer's hot breath ghosted over Emilio's glans. "Want me to kiss it and make it better?"

Emilio moaned and spread his legs, giving Spencer room to work. A hot tongue lapped at the head of his dick, and then Spencer opened his lips wide and dropped them down, taking Emilio in deep right from the start.

"Fuck, Spence," Emilio groaned. He tangled his fingers in Spencer's hair and encouraged his movements. "Like that. Just like that."

He looked down and moaned at the sight of Spencer curled over his lap, his head bobbing as he massaged Emilio's balls with one hand and stroked his own dick with the other. Underneath the conservative clothes, fancy college job, and sweet blushes lived a voracious sex kitten. And Emilio thought he might have been the first man to discover that. Damn, was he ever lucky.

"Love you, Spence," he said. He massaged Spencer's head and thrust his hips up in small increments. "You ready for me?" he asked, but he already knew the answer, knew Spencer loved the taste of him. Spencer moaned and sucked harder. Yup, lucky. "Ungh," he moaned as his pleasure peaked, then he arched his neck, closed his eyes, and stilled as his cock pulsed into Spencer's eager mouth.

"C'mere," he said just as soon as he was done. His muscles were languid, brain a little fuzzy, but he knew what he wanted.

Spencer blinked up at him, his tongue still lapping at Emilio's dick. Fuck, that was hot. He lay back on the bed, his legs still hanging over the edge, and pulled Spencer over to him. "Wanna touch you," he explained, and then he encouraged Spencer to straddle his hips and reached for his rigid shaft, wrapping his fingers around it.

"Oh!" Spencer cried out.

"That's it. Come on," Emilio encouraged as he pulled.

Spencer planted his palms on Emilio's chest and thrust up into his hand, grunting and moaning. It didn't take long before he was speeding up and then his eyes flew open, looking right at Emilio as he gasped and came, his hot seed spilling over Emilio's fist. Emilio stroked him through it and then pulled him down for a soft kiss.

When Spencer's body relaxed and the kisses came slower and slower, Emilio rolled him onto the bed and pulled the covers over him. "Call me later," he whispered, kissing his temple before getting up.

"'Kay," Spencer mumbled, sounding sleepy. He yawned, closed his eyes, and cuddled under the blanket. "Love you."

So sweet. His man was so sweet. Emilio smiled, feeling

light, happy, and grateful as he started his day.

EMILIO WAS thirty feet off the ground, running wires across beams when his phone rang, so he didn't answer it. When he was safely on his feet, he called Spencer back, getting his voice mail. They traded calls all day, never connecting.

When he was almost done for the day, Emilio found a quiet corner and called Spencer again. "Hey, *cariño*, I know you got another class and then that meeting, so we can talk tonight, okay?" He lowered his voice and added, "Thanks for this morning. Been thinking about how much I wanna return the favor all day."

He disconnected the line and smirked at the thought of Spencer listening to his message and getting aroused. That cut both ways, though, because turning Spencer on ramped Emilio right up. He groaned as his dick started to fill and reached down to adjust himself.

"Yo, this is a job site! Keep your hands out of your pants, bro."

Emilio rolled his eyes as he turned around, flipped his brother off, and said, "Whatever."

"So what favor you gonna return?" Henry asked.

"You really wanna know?" Emilio asked, arching his eyebrows.

"Was it hot?"

"Fuck yeah," Emilio groaned, his eyes rolling back in his head for a whole different reason.

"Then tell me." Henry walked closer.

Not wanting to broadcast his sex life to the whole crew, Emilio darted his gaze around to make sure they were alone. "Spencer can suck like a dream."

"Yeah?" Henry sounded envious. "Does he swallow?"

"Uh-huh." Emilio nodded.

"Fuck! You're lucky."

"Stacy doesn't swallow?"

"Nah." Henry shrugged. "I mean, I ain't ever asked her or nothing, but no. It feels good, right? I bet it feels good."

Figuring the question was rhetorical, Emilio ignored it and said, "Why haven't you asked her?"

"I don't know, man. I feel bad enough asking her to put her mouth on my dick. Asking her to let me come in her mouth seems like too much."

Emilio chuckled and punched Henry in the arm. "Why would you feel bad? She probably likes it."

"You think so?" Henry asked disbelievingly.

"Sure. Why not? I like it."

"Well, yeah, but getting a blow job isn't the same as giving one."

"I meant I like giving them."

Henry's eyebrows shot up. "Seriously?"

"Oh, yeah," Emilio said, a little growl sneaking in as he

thought about how much he enjoyed taking Spencer into his mouth and making him shake and come. "Love it."

"Huh," Henry said, absorbing the information.

"What're you guys talkin' about?" Martin, Emilio's second oldest brother, asked as he walked up to them.

Emilio locked gazes with Henry and raised one eyebrow in question. The two of them were closer in age than their older siblings. They had shared a room until Emilio graduated high school and they had both moved out of their parents' house. Those things meant they usually shared more with each other than with their other brothers, and definitely more than with their sister.

Henry was the first person Emilio had come out to, the one he had gone to when he had questions about beating off. And Emilio had stayed up late many nights, listening to Henry whisper details about his early sexual exploits. Being best friends with your brother meant there wasn't a whole lot off-limits. But that didn't mean they wanted to share with the rest of their siblings.

"Nothing," they said simultaneously, and then they started giggling.

"What?" Martin asked. "Tell me."

"Nothing, man, seriously," Henry said.

"Yeah, you don't wanna know," Emilio agreed. "What's up?"

"Tell me. You two are always whispering about stuff. I wanna know."

Emilio laughed. "We weren't whispering, Martin. We were just talkin'."

"About what?" Martin crossed his arms over his chest, trying to look intimidating. It had stopped working on Emilio when he had outgrown Martin, along with his other brothers. It hadn't ever worked on Henry.

"Nothin' you're interested in," Henry said.

"I'm interested," Martin insisted. "Come on, tell me."

Knowing his brother well enough to realize he wasn't going to back down, Emilio relented and said, "Blow jobs. You happy now?"

Martin looked around quickly. "What about them?"

Henry flicked his gaze to Emilio, his eyebrows raised in question. Emilio shrugged.

"What?" Martin demanded.

"Does Rosa swallow when she goes down on you?"

"What the fuck?" Martin shouted and smacked the back of Henry's head. "That's my wife you're talking about!"

"Ow!" Henry rubbed the injured spot. "That's why we don't tell you shit, man! That hurt. Fuck."

Martin scowled and turned his attention to Emilio, who reflexively jumped out of reach and threw his hands up.

"Chill out, man. You made us tell you!"

"Made you tell him what?" Raul asked as he walked up.

"Nothing," the three other brothers answered in unison.

"What?" Raul asked, snapping his gaze from one of them to the other. "Tell me."

CARDENO C.

"Man, it's like a fucking rerun," Emilio said.

"What does that mean?" Raul snapped.

"It means we already fell for this question with Martin, and then when I told him, he hit me!" Henry shouted.

"You hit Henry?" Raul asked, taking on his protective oldest brother tone.

"Don't be such a pussy, Henry, it didn't hurt," Martin yelled.

"Why'd you hit him?" Raul demanded.

"'Cause he's a perverted little fuck!" Martin answered.

"You having a flashback to when we were kids?" Emilio mock-whispered to Henry.

"Yeah," Henry answered with a chuckle. "And you're just as uptight now as you were then." He lobbed the insult at Martin as he jumped back, making sure there was plenty of space between them.

Martin lunged for Henry. Emilio jumped between them. Raul grabbed Martin's shoulders, holding him back. After a few tense seconds with all of them breathing hard, Martin started chuckling. Henry followed, snorting out a laugh. Then Emilio and Raul joined in at the same time. They leaned on each other, all four brothers laughing and gasping for air.

"Hey, you guys wanna go get a beer and shoot some pool?" Martin asked when they'd all calmed down. "We haven't done that in forever."

"Sure thing," Henry answered, throwing his arm over Martin's shoulder and giving him a friendly squeeze.

"I'll call Jim," Raul said. "Alicia likes when we include him in shit."

"Cool," Emilio answered. "We going to Shooters?"

"Yeah," Martin answered.

"I caught a ride in today," Henry said. "Can I get a lift with you?"

"Sure," Emilio answered. They all walked to their trucks, and Emilio waited until they were climbing in before loudly saying, "Hey, Henry, now we can finish our conversation."

"You're sick fucks!" Martin shouted.

Emilio slammed his door, looked at Henry, and started laughing all over again.

# CHAPTER 16

IT HAD been the Friday to end all Fridays. A full schedule of classes, two last-minute classroom changes because of the construction, and a line out the door for office hours, topped off by a department meeting. Even with all of that, Spencer had stayed happy all day. All week, really. Heck, he'd upgrade that to a month, because that was how long Emilio had been in his life.

"I want details," Maria Lee said as she followed Spencer into his office after the meeting. She kicked the door closed behind her.

"Details?" Spencer asked in confusion. "You were sitting right next to me. Weren't you paying attention?"

"I wasn't talking about the meeting," she said. "Not that I was paying attention in there. Who calls a meeting on a Friday afternoon? Serves them right if they have to repeat everything." She waved her hand in dismissal and flopped into Spencer's chair. "Anyway, I want details about whatever your man did in bed that has you floating around and grinning like a loon."

Spencer's cheeks heated. He ducked his head and

gathered his papers, then straightened them before sliding them into his briefcase.

"You're no fun," Maria said. "You never tell me anything. If I had a guy who looked like that in bed, I'd give you every detail."

Spencer knew firsthand that Maria had no qualms about sharing way too much information, even when she didn't have a man who was anywhere near as beautiful as Emilio in her bed, and even when Spencer begged her to have mercy on him and stop.

"You have a great imagination, Maria," he said as he buckled his case. "Just take whatever you're thinking and double the heat. That should give you the idea."

"Ohhh, you are evil!" Maria said with a laugh.

Spencer waggled his eyebrows. "How're things going with Thom Bramfield?" he asked.

"I gave up on Coach Confusing," she announced. "At first I thought he was being gentlemanly, then I thought he was doing that whole out-of-reach thing to drag me in, but at this point, I'm pretty sure he actually means it when he says he just wants to be friends." She scoffed in disgust. "Can you believe that?"

"Friends is nice," Spencer said as he walked around his desk, heading for the door. "What's wrong with friends?"

"I have enough friends," Maria said, getting up from her chair. "What I need is a good lay. I'm thinking of trying chicks."

Spencer halted and panned his gaze over to her. "Okay, first, I'm pretty sure we're not supposed to say chicks. And second, you can't just switch teams. It doesn't work that way."

"Hey, some of the best sex of my life was with this chick I roomed with in college." She paused. "See? I can say chick and it sounds fine."

"You slept with a woman?" Spencer asked in surprise.

"More than one," Maria answered haughtily. "Hot, right?"

Spencer gaped.

"Okay, maybe not to you," she said. "But trust me on this: it's hot."

"You had sex with women because you thought guys would like it?" Spencer said incredulously.

"Of course not!" Maria answered, sounding completely affronted. "I fuck women when I want to fuck women and I fuck men when I want to fuck men."

"You're bi?"

"Sure," Maria said, like it was the most obvious thing in the world. "Everyone's bi. Most people just don't want to admit it."

"Uh, no. I'm pretty sure that's not true," Spencer demurred.

"Fine," Maria relented with a sigh. "Everyone except you."

Spencer would have argued, but just then a knock sounded on his door.

"Should we make really loud sex noises so whoever's out

there thinks we're doing it?" Maria asked excitedly.

"Sometimes I don't know if you're a student or a professor," Spencer said, shaking his head.

"Thanks!" Maria responded.

"It wasn't a compliment," he said as he reached for the doorway.

"Says you."

He stared at her and shook his head as he opened the door. "Seriously, Maria, you sound like—"

"Hello." Peter's voice stopped Spencer midsentence.

He swung his head around to see his ex-boyfriend standing in his office doorway.

"Uh, hello. Hi. What... Hi." Spencer snapped his mouth shut to stop his embarrassing rambling. He was taking a few breaths, trying to get his wits about him, when Maria strode up and stood next to him.

"Hello, Maria. It's a pleasure to see you again. How have you been?"

"Peter," Maria said. "The pleasure is all yours. Why are you here?"

Peter scowled and crossed his arms over his chest. "I see you're still a raging bitch."

She mirrored his stance, hiking her breasts up until they almost touched her chin. "Takes one to know one."

"Okay, the teenager impression is not helping," Spencer hissed at her. Then he turned his attention to Peter and said, "Look, I don't mean to be rude, but—" He took a deep breath.

"Why *are* you here?"

"Last weekend didn't work out, so I thought we'd try it tonight," Peter said.

"Try what?" Maria growled, her eyes squinting dangerously.

"I wasn't talking to you!" Peter snapped at her. "I was talking to Spencer."

Wow. Things were getting more awkward by the moment. "Maria, don't you have somewhere to be?" Spencer asked, trying to separate her from Peter before she ripped his head off.

"Where?" Maria asked him.

"Anywhere but here?" Peter offered sarcastically.

Maria opened her mouth but Spencer spoke first and said, "Peter, seriously, what are you doing here?"

"I just told you. I'm here so we can have that dinner we talked about last week."

"You agreed to go to dinner with this dickless jerk?" Maria screeched.

Peter's face turned a disturbing shade of crimson. "Now, you listen here, you little—"

"Nobody is going to dinner with anybody," Spencer said hurriedly.

"But—" Peter started.

Spencer's phone rang. "Excuse me," he said, opening the front pocket of his briefcase and reaching for his phone. "That's probably Emilio. We've been playing phone tag all day."

"Who's Emilio?" Peter asked.

"His boyfriend," Maria answered smugly. "His super hot, super hung boyfriend."

"Very classy, Maria," Peter said. "It's a wonder you're still single."

Spencer turned his back on them and answered his phone. "Hello."

"Hey, Spence," Emilio said. "Am I interrupting you during your meeting?"

Hearing that deep, warm voice helped ease the tension that had been gathering in Spencer's belly. "No, we're all done. I was just about to head home. Are you there?"

"No, my brothers and I went to shoot some pool. Come join us."

"Oh. No, no, that's okay. I don't want to interrupt your bonding time." He tried to keep the disappointment out of his voice. He had been looking forward to racing home and being with Emilio.

"Bonding time?" Emilio chuckled. "Spence, I work with my brothers. I see them every day. Jim's here too. Come on, please? I want you to get to know them. You haven't even met Martin and Henry yet."

The idea of meeting Emilio's family was still a little daunting, but Raul had seemed nice during the brief time they'd spent together, and Spencer liked Jim a lot. Besides, Emilio's family was an important part of his life, which meant it was important to Spencer too.

"Okay. I'll come join you. Where are you?"

"Shooters. You know the place?"

Spencer tucked his phone between his shoulder and his ear and reached into his bag for a piece of paper and a pen. "Shooters? No. Where is it?"

He scribbled the address down, repeated it to make sure he had it right, and told Emilio he'd be there soon. Then he dropped his phone into his bag and tried to stay calm as he turned back to Peter. Well, Peter and Maria, who was shooting daggers at Peter with her eyes.

"Peter, I'm sorry, but I have plans, and besides I—"

"I heard," Peter snapped. "Is that the guy from the restaurant the other night? He hasn't broken up with you yet?"

"Seriously?" Maria shouted. "Who the hell do you think you are?"

"Okay!" Spencer said loudly. "Okay. That's enough." He put his arm on Maria's back and looked meaningfully at Peter, nudging his chin toward the doorway. "Let's go."

Once all three of them were in the hallway, he locked the door and started walking toward the stairwell, Maria on one side of him and Peter on the other. They barely fit in the hallway, all three of them shoulder to shoulder, but Peter and Maria were both too stubborn to budge.

"We need to talk," Peter said.

"No, you don't," Maria responded.

"Oh, for God's sake, will you please shut up!" Peter shouted.

"I'm an atheist," Maria said.

"Figures," Peter grumbled.

"What is that supposed to mean?" Maria replied.

Spencer ignored both of them as they all hustled down the stairs and out of the building, then he asked Peter, "Are you in visitor parking?"

"Yes."

"Okay, well, Maria and I are in the staff lot and it's in the opposite direction, so..."

"We need to talk, Spencer."

"Peter," Spencer sighed. "I don't think there's anything left to say, okay?"

"Yeah, Peter!" Maria jumped in, sounding joyful. "There's nothing left to say."

"Maria, I've got this," Spencer said firmly. "You can go ahead. I'll call you later."

"No, thanks. I'll wait." She jutted her hip out, crossed her arms over her chest, and glared at Peter.

Spencer rolled his eyes, took a deep breath, and said, "Peter, listen, I need to go. I'm meeting—"

"Emilio," Peter said the name like it was dirty. "I heard. When can we talk?"

Not wanting to embarrass Peter, Spencer looked at Maria and said, "Give us a minute, okay?"

It seemed as if she was going to protest, but Spencer

looked at her pleadingly and she said, "Fine. But I'll be right over there." Then she stomped off to a light post not too far away, leaned against it, and continued glaring at Peter.

"I can come over after dinner," Peter offered.

"No." Spencer shook his head. "We've been done for a long time. You moved on. I moved on. I don't see the point of rehashing everything."

"It's not rehashing. I've been giving it a lot of thought, and I think we can—"

"Spencer!" Maria called out. "Emilio's waiting for you!"

"She's right." Spencer looked at the man who once held the power to send him into a tailspin, gave him a kind smile, and said, "Take care of yourself, Peter." Then he walked away.

"IF YOU stare at the door one more time, I'm going to hit you in the head with my cue," Martin said to Emilio.

"Leave him alone, man," Raul responded. "*Hermanito* is waiting for his professor."

"Can't he wait without staring at the door like a lovesick puppy?"

"That's nothing," Raul scoffed. "You should have seen him when he was stalking the man's office. It was the sorriest damn thing I've ever seen."

"I'm sure he didn't stalk Spencer's office," Jim said

reasonably.

"Yeah, he did," Henry disagreed.

"Yeah, I did," Emilio confirmed. "You've met him. Can you blame me?" He looked from Jim to Raul. "He's adorable, right? Did you see his dimples? And he's nice and smart and—"

"Ah, man." Martin shook his head. "Cut it out. You're making my stomach hurt." He looked at the other men and asked, "Were any of us ever that sickeningly sweet?"

"Not me," Henry responded before taking a swig of his beer.

"Me either," Raul said.

"I still feel that way when I think about your sister," Jim replied.

Emilio held his beer bottle up and tipped Jim's. "Hear, hear, man." He took a sip and then glanced at the door again. This time, he saw Spencer walk in, squinting as his eyes adjusted to the dim lighting. Emilio raised his hand in a wave and Spencer smiled brightly. He rushed over to their table.

"Hey, *cariño*," Emilio said quietly as he cupped Spencer's nape and gave him an affectionate squeeze. "How was your day?"

"Better now." Spencer rubbed his hand over Emilio's chest and looked up at him, his pretty brown eyes twinkling, his dimples showing.

Emilio wanted to strip him naked and bend him over the nearest flat surface, but he was pretty sure that'd get them kicked out of the pool hall.

"Probably get you arrested too, bro," Henry said, bumping his shoulder.

"Did I say that out loud?" Emilio asked in surprise.

"Yup." Henry winked as he pressed his bottle to his lips and tilted it up.

"Yes," Spencer said at the same time, his cheeks bright red. "You did."

"Sorry, *cariño*," Emilio mumbled. "You do that to me."

Spencer flushed and smiled, looking embarrassed but pleased.

"Ain't you gonna introduce me to your man?" Henry asked.

Emilio put his hand on Spencer's back and drew him close. "Spencer, this is my brother, Henry. Henry, Spencer."

"Nice to finally meet you," Spencer said, reaching his hand out. "I've heard a lot about you."

"If it was bad, it was probably a lie," Henry responded, taking Spencer's hand in his and shaking it. "Or maybe not." He winked. Martin walked up, and Henry added, "We've heard a lot about you too. In fact, we were just talking about you before we came here. Ain't that right, Martin?"

"What're you... Oh, man, gross. Cut it out!" Martin said. He shook his head, as if he was trying to clear away a horrible thought, and then he reached for Spencer's hand. "Martin Sanchez. Good to meet you."

Spencer looked at Emilio, his eyebrows scrunched together, confusion mapped on his face. "Oh, uh, nice to meet you too." He shook Martin's hand and blinked quickly.

"Ignore them, Spencer," Emilio said and glared at Henry. "They're just being assholes and they're gonna stop right now. Ain't that right, Henry?"

"Sorry," Henry said, not sounding at all sorry, then he wandered back to the pool table with Martin on his heels. Emilio heard a smack followed by an "Ow!" so he figured Martin had gone after Henry again. It was deserved, so he ignored them.

"Your family is really different from mine," Spencer observed, his eyes wide.

Worried they had upset Spencer, Emilio said, "They mean well. We just kid each other a lot, but I can tell them to stop."

"No, don't." Spencer grasped Emilio's wrist. "It's nice that you're all so close." He glanced at Emilio's brothers and sighed longingly. "You have a wonderful family."

Emilio hated that Spencer had drawn the short straw when it came to families, but he hoped maybe one day Spencer would feel like part of his family. If he knew his mother, she'd make sure of it.

"Hey, Spencer!" Raul marched up, grabbed Spencer's palm with one hand and clapped his shoulder with the other. "Good to see you again. You want a beer?"

Spencer hesitated for a second and then he seemed to relax in response to Raul's jovial smile. "No, I'm good for right now. Thank you."

"How about a soda?" Jim asked as he approached Spencer. "I'm heading up to the bar to get a refill anyway."

"A soda would be great. Thanks, Jim," Spencer said. "How've you been?"

"Good. Alicia and I had a great time the other night. She hasn't stopped talking about how much she wants to have you and Emilio over for dinner so you can meet the kids. We'll have to compare calendars before we leave and get something on the books."

"Sounds great," Spencer said.

"Good." Jim nodded, seeming pleased that had been decided. He patted Spencer on the shoulder and said, "Be right back." Then he and Raul walked toward the bar.

"So," Emilio said once he was finally alone with Spencer. "Busy—"

"Spencer," a man called out as he approached them from behind. "We need to talk."

All the color drained from Spencer's face at the sound of that voice. He flipped around and said, "Peter! What are you doing here?"

So this was Peter the ex-boyfriend. Emilio looked him up and down and decided he wasn't impressed. The man's face was pinched, his eyes beady, and he wore his hair in a comb-over, like he was thinning up top but trying to hide it. It never worked when guys did that, and Emilio always wondered why they didn't just cut it short and own it. He knew a lot of good-looking bald guys.

"Like I said," Peter responded, "we need to talk."

Spencer's posture stiffened. "I'm sorry," he said to Emilio. "I'll just be a minute."

"You need me to get rid of him?" Emilio asked quietly.

The corner of Spencer's mouth turned up. "Tempting as that sounds, no. I need to deal with this."

"Are you sure?" Emilio asked. "I wouldn't mind." He clenched his fists and cracked his knuckles. "At all."

Spencer smiled broadly. "I'm sure."

"Spencer," Peter said, his voice louder. "I'm waiting."

With a flinch, Spencer turned around and walked over to Peter. Emilio heard him say, "Keep your voice down." After that, they spoke too quietly for Emilio to make out the words, but he could tell from their facial expressions that they weren't talking about anything good.

"Who is that?" Henry said from behind Emilio.

He looked back over his shoulder. "Spencer's ex. Guy's a total asshole."

"Should we take care of him?" Henry asked immediately.

"Spencer said he wanted to handle it himself," Emilio answered before turning his attention back to Spencer and Peter.

"Then let's stop staring at them." Henry tugged on Emilio's shoulder. "Come on, we have a game to finish."

Emilio grudgingly followed his brother to the pool table.

"Martin, you're up," Henry said as they approached.

"Who's the guy talking to Spencer?" Martin asked as he

picked up his cue. "Four ball, side pocket." He lined up his cue stick, took the shot, and missed.

"Spencer's ex-boyfriend," Emilio said, glancing over at the two men again.

"Huh," Martin responded. "Henry, it's your shot." He walked over to Emilio and followed his gaze. "Should we go take care of him?" he asked.

Emilio heard the balls connecting, indicating that Henry had taken his turn.

"We're not in the fuckin' Mafia," Henry said, as if he hadn't just suggested the same thing. "Besides, Spencer said he wanted to handle it himself. You're up, Emilio."

Emilio picked up his cue and walked over to the side of the table that would give him a good view of Spencer.

"I don't like his body language," Martin said, still staring at Peter.

"I don't either," Emilio responded. The man was scowling, his face contorted in anger, and he kept throwing his arms around. Emilio leaned over the table and lined up his shot. "Eight ball, left corner of his pocket," he said. Then he hit the ball hard, bounced it over the edge of the table, and sent it flying, right into Peter's groin. The asshole cried out and dropped to his knees.

Spencer spun around and stared at Emilio.

He shrugged and smirked.

"You missed," Martin said.

"Nah, I think he landed his shot right on target," Henry

responded as he looked at Peter crouched on the ground, cupping his balls with his hands.

"No. He said corner pocket." Martin tilted the bottom of his beer bottle in Peter's direction. "That was a zipper shot," he argued.

"I said left corner *of his* pocket," Emilio corrected. He leaned back against the pool table and crossed his arms over his chest. "The inside corner is probably up against the zipper. I nailed it."

"True." Martin shrugged and took a swig of his beer. "It was hard to see from this angle."

All three of them watched as Spencer crouched next to Peter, seemingly trying to help him.

"You gonna get in trouble?" Henry asked.

"Probably not. Spence is really forgiving." Emilio chewed on his bottom lip. "But if he's pissed, I'll just do that thing I told you about earlier until he gets over it."

"Yeah, good call," Henry said.

Spencer glanced up and met Emilio's gaze. Emilio raised his eyebrows in question, and Spencer grinned for just a second before grasping Peter's arm and helping him up.

Though he didn't have the details, Emilio knew Peter had been an asshole to Spencer when they were together and that Peter was the one who had ended the relationship. He could understand why Peter would regret walking away; hell, if he lost Spencer, he'd probably feel nothing but regret for the rest of his life. But following him to a public place for the second weekend in a row and trying to embarrass him was a dick move, plain and simple. And yelling instead of getting on his knees and begging was just stupid. Yet despite all that, Spencer was still trying to help Peter up off the floor, still being kind.

Emilio's heart warmed as he looked at his man; Spencer really was the sweetest guy alive. "Actually," Emilio said. "I'm gonna do that thing either way."

"I don't want to know," Martin muttered.

# CHAPTER 17

THOUGH SPENCER would have thought it impossible, his day had just gotten weirder: the "everyone is bisexual" conversation with Maria, followed by Peter showing up at his office, and then Maria and Peter fighting like they were teenagers. Well, the last one was actually somewhat par for the course. Maria had never liked Peter, and Peter had never liked anybody who didn't think he was wonderful.

But the weirdest part of all was that Peter had listened to him repeat the pool hall address and then followed him there. Dismissing Spencer's text cancelling dinner was one thing, but coming after him when he knew full well that Spencer was meeting his date was just plain rude. Spencer had tried explaining that very thing to Peter, but he had refused to listen and instead ranted endlessly about how they should get back together but have an open relationship. Apparently, Peter considered that the solution to all their problems.

Spencer had been trying to let him down gently, trying to say goodbye once and for all, but Peter got angry, well, angrier, and then a pool ball came out of nowhere and hit him right in the crotch. The next thing Spencer knew, Peter was writhing on the floor and Emilio and his brothers were looking right at him.

He flicked his gaze from the cue stick in Emilio's hand over to his handsome face, taking note of his self-satisfied expression, and the pieces fell together: Emilio had intentionally hit Peter with the ball. Spencer snorted in amusement and had to force himself to curl his lips over his teeth to stop smiling.

"Are you okay?" he asked Peter. "Here, I'll help you up." He knelt, put one hand on Peter's back and the other on his elbow, and supported him as he stood.

"This is why civilized people don't spend their time pushing little balls into little holes over and over again," Peter grumbled. "Not to mention the fact that it smells terrible in here." He twitched his nose, his expression sour and put-upon. "Let's go."

Peter grabbed Spencer's wrist and tried pulling him toward the door.

"I'm not leaving with you," Spencer said as he dug in his heels. "Haven't you been listening to me? I told you, I'm here with my boyfriend."

"And I told you that I'd take you back," Peter said. When he wasn't able to make Spencer budge, he sighed and said, "Okay, fine, I'll admit I should have thought of trying an open relationship before we broke up, but I was very frustrated at the time. The important thing is, I thought of it now." He paused and looked at Spencer expectantly.

"Uh," Spencer said, not sure how to respond.

"I accept your apology," Peter said. "Let's go."

"I didn't apologize!" Spencer hissed, trying to keep his voice down. He shook Peter's hand off. "This is ridiculous."

"Spencer, here's your sod…" Jim stopped in his tracks and looked back and forth between Spencer and Peter, a soda in each of his hands. "Is everything okay?"

"Terrific, now we're going to have a scene," Peter said disgruntledly. "How awkward."

Spencer jerked his gaze over to him and dropped his jaw in shock. The awkward scene had started when Peter had shown up in his office, and things had degenerated from there. How did he not realize that? Once again, Spencer wondered what he had ever seen in the man.

"Spencer?" Jim repeated.

"Oh, uh, I'm fine." Spencer shook off his confusion over Peter's behavior and reached for the cup. "Peter was just leaving. Thank you for the soda."

"Look, Spencer, I said I was sorry," Peter said. Spencer didn't bother pointing out that he hadn't said any such thing. "You can't actually want to be with him instead of me," he added haughtily as he pointed his thumb in Jim's direction.

Spencer immediately turned to Jim, wanting to apologize for Peter's nasty words, for his inaccurate assumption, pretty much for anything and everything relating to Peter, but then Jim started laughing hysterically.

"Wait, you think we're together?" He pointed back and

forth between Spencer and himself. "Oh, that's rich! I can't wait to tell Alicia I passed as gay next time she accuses me of having no fashion sense." He paused and snapped his gaze to Spencer. "Oh, uh, sorry. That's not rude, is it?"

"I thought you said you were meeting your boyfriend!" Peter shouted accusingly. "I should have known this was another one of your elaborate games, Spencer." He grabbed Spencer's shoulders. "Didn't I make it clear that I do not appreciate your nonsense? If you insist on—"

"Peter, please stop," Spencer said, trying to wiggle free. "I'm not playing games with you. I'm not getting back together with you. I'm asking you to leave."

"Why?" Peter sneered. "So you can spend time with your imaginary boyfriend?"

Spencer heard Emilio's heavy footsteps right before his deep voice boomed from behind him. "The only thing I'm imagining is kicking your ass if you don't get your fucking hands off Spencer right fucking now!"

Peter stepped back and gulped. "Who are you?" he asked, looking wide-eyed and a little pale.

"I'm Spencer's boyfriend," Emilio said as he walked right up to Spencer and rubbed his hands over his arms. "Are you okay, *cariño*?" he asked softly. "Did he hurt you?"

"No." Spencer shook his head. "I'm fine." He dropped his chin, feeling his cheeks heat. "God, this is embarrassing. I'm so sorry. Your brothers must think—"

"Wait," Peter said. "*This* is your boyfriend?" he asked

disbelievingly.

Spencer knew he probably should have been offended, but he understood the sentiment. Emilio was stunning and kind and talented and it was hard to believe he was real, let alone that he wanted to be with him. But he did. Spencer still didn't know why Emilio wanted him, but he knew Emilio wouldn't lie to him. Not about that or anything else.

"Yes," Emilio answered Peter's question. "We live together. You had your chance with him and you blew it. Spencer is mine now, so back the fuck off."

"Oh, I get it," Peter said condescendingly after a beat. "You moved him into your house, is that it? You're supporting him and you think that makes him your boyfriend." He laughed cruelly. "I thought if nothing else, you were more intelligent than this. Be real, Spencer. He's using you!"

"Using me?" Spencer repeated, trying to process what Peter meant and quickly deciding he didn't care. But before he could say that, Peter kept talking.

"Yes, he's trying to get every cent out of you he can and then he'll disappear into the night. It's a good thing I'm here to save you from yourself."

"Peter, you've really gone too far," Spencer said through gritted teeth. "I won't have you insulting Emilio. You need to leave. Now."

"You can't be serious," Peter said to Spencer, and then he glared at Emilio. "I'm not naïve like Spencer. I know you're using him for money!"

"Oh, man," Emilio said with a chuckle. "You got it all wrong. Hell, with the amount of time I've spent remodeling Spencer's house for free, I'm the one paying him." He shook his head. "I'm not with Spencer for money." Emilio looked right at Peter. "I'm with him for the great sex."

Everyone was quiet for a few seconds, and then Jim cleared his throat, breaking the silence. "Well, then," he said. "I suppose that's the end of that. Peter, I suggest you leave now."

Though he looked shaken, Peter refused to back down. "This is a public establishment; you can't make me leave," he said to Jim.

"No, I can't," Jim admitted. "I'm just making a friendly suggestion because the two men walking over from the pool table right now and the guy storming over from the bar? Those are Emilio's brothers. They're pretty protective of their family, and they include Spencer on that list. Seeing as how you just had your hands all over him, I would think you'd want to leave now and hope you never run into them again."

Peter looked around the room, seemingly taking in the three Sanchez brothers approaching from all directions. He raised his pointer finger in the air, opened his mouth, then clapped it shut and scurried out of the bar. A few seconds later, the three brothers surrounded them.

"What happened?" Martin asked.

"Are you okay, Spencer?" Henry said at the same time.

"Who was that guy?" Raul demanded as he stared at Peter's retreating form.

"I'm fine," Spencer said, forcing himself to look Emilio's brothers in the eyes even though he wanted to crawl under the nearest table and hide. "I am so sorry for—" He waved his hand at the spot Peter had occupied. "All of that."

"You don't need to apologize for that asshole," Emilio growled. "That shit wasn't your fault."

"That guy coming back?" Raul asked.

"I sincerely doubt it," Jim responded.

"Good," Raul said as he started walking toward the pool table. "Who's up? Or should we just start a new game?"

"New game," Martin said, trailing after him.

"Fine by me," Henry agreed.

"I'm going to sit this one out," Jim said as he followed them. "Alicia will be home soon, so I'm only going to stay a few more minutes."

As soon as they were gone, Emilio gazed down at Spencer. "Are you sure you're okay, *cariño*?" he asked.

"I'm sure. I really am sorry about all this drama. I have no idea what got into Peter all of a sudden."

"I do," Emilio said. "He wants you back. I don't blame the guy, but you're mine and I ain't giving you up, so he's shit out of luck."

Spencer beamed. "I think he got the message."

"Good."

"So," Spencer said quietly. "You're using me for sex, are

you?"

Emilio's cheeks darkened. "No! He was just pissing me
off and I, uh—"

"I guess that means I better put out, huh?"

Emilio's eyes widened in surprise, then he dragged his
gaze over Spencer's body and shivered. There was no way
to mistake Emilio's feelings. He not only told Spencer that
he wanted to be with him, but he showed him every day,
through his actions, through his expressions, and, right at
that second, through the little whimper that escaped him. It
made Spencer feel strong, knowing he could affect this man
so deeply. And that strength, that confidence, made him trust
Emilio even more.

He stepped close, leaned into Emilio's ear, and dropped
his voice as he said, "How many times do you think I can
make you come before you pass out?"

"Let's go home," Emilio said hoarsely. "I want you naked.
Right now." He draped his arm over Spencer's shoulders and
hustled them toward the door.

"Don't you want to say goodbye to your brothers and
Jim?" Spencer asked, his voice full of amusement.

"Hey, we're takin' off," Emilio yelled over his shoulder.
"See you guys later." Without waiting for a response, he
rushed them out of the bar.

EMILIO DROVE home in a haze of lust. Damn, his man was hot. Watching Spencer's confidence grow and knowing he'd played a part in it was a major turn-on. Listening to his conservative, buttoned-up professor talk dirty had Emilio hard so fast he ached.

Spencer's car was already in the driveway by the time he got home. He pulled up to the curb and raced inside, groaning when he saw a trail of discarded clothing leading to the bedroom. Walking down the hallway, he picked up each of Spencer's shoes, his vest, his shirt, and then, in the bedroom doorway, his pants. Emilio added the pants to the pile he was carrying, then he stepped into the room to find Spencer wearing only his briefs.

The two of them stared at each other, and it felt like the air was electric. Then, before Emilio could say anything, Spencer flew over to him, knocked the clothes out of his hands, and climbed him like a tree.

"Want you so much," Spencer mumbled as he kissed Emilio's neck and rubbed up against him. He fumbled with Emilio's pants and dropped to his knees, nuzzling Emilio's groin through his jeans as he got them open. He pulled the jeans and briefs down, moaning when Emilio's dick bobbed out and made contact with his face. "God, Emilio," Spencer moaned. He wrapped his hand around Emilio's shaft and rubbed his cheek against it, like a cat. "You're so beautiful. Every part of you." He dipped lower and started sucking on Emilio's balls.

"Spence," Emilio said, his voice sounding gravelly with arousal. He threaded his fingers through Spencer's hair and nudged his head back so their eyes could connect. "You know you don't gotta do this, right? I was just giving that asshole a hard time. I ain't with you just for sex."

Without moving his gaze from Emilio's, Spencer licked his way up his dick. "I know," he said. "I'm not with you for that reason either." He swirled his tongue around Emilio's crown. "But you like it, right?"

Emilio was breathing so hard he thought he was going to pass out. "Huh?" he asked, his brain too fuzzy with arousal to be able to process the question.

"Sex with me," Spencer clarified. "You like it?" Then he licked his lips and dropped them over Emilio's dick, sucking him down.

"Ungh!" Emilio groaned and bucked. "Spence!"

Spencer popped off his dick. "Do you?" he asked.

Emilio had to force himself to focus and remember what they had been discussing. "Yeah, Spence, Jesus," he panted. "'Course I like it." He paused and looked at Spencer, really looked at him, his swollen lips, his flushed skin, his wide pupils, his hair, disheveled from where Emilio had been tugging it. "You are the sexiest man I ever met. Ain't nobody ever made me feel the way you do."

The answer seemed to satisfy Spencer because he grinned up at Emilio and then went back to work licking his balls, swirling his tongue all over his dick, and eventually taking him into his mouth and moving up and down, sucking him while he stroked his hand over Emilio's saliva-slick skin. It didn't take long for him to reach the edge, not with Spencer going to town on him like there was nothing he'd rather do than get on his knees and suck Emilio's dick.

"Love you, Spence," Emilio moaned. "Oh God." He gulped and bucked.

Spencer pulled his mouth off but kept stroking Emilio's shaft. "Do it," he begged. "Show me how I make you feel." Then he looked right into Emilio's eyes as he dropped his jaw and held his open mouth right in front of Emilio's glans, never slowing the pace of his strokes.

"Jesus," Emilio gasped. "Uh-huh, uh-huh." He thrust forward and shot so hard the world went fuzzy around the edges. When he saw his seed collect on Spencer's tongue, his entire body trembled, the orgasm going on and on until his knees buckled and he collapsed onto the floor.

Emilio stared as Spencer closed his mouth, swallowed, and moaned. Then he licked his lips, like he wanted to collect any remnant of Emilio he had missed. Not able to think, barely able to breathe, Emilio lunged, slanted his mouth over Spencer's, and held him close as he kissed and licked and sucked on his lips.

"Emilio," Spencer sighed happily. He wrapped his legs around Emilio's waist, climbed onto his lap, and gently combed his fingers through Emilio's hair as he sucked on his tongue. Though Spencer's dick was hard as steel, pressing against Emilio's belly, he made no move to get off, didn't ask Emilio to return the favor, choosing instead to cuddle and kiss and bask.

It had taken Emilio by surprise at first, how giving Spencer was in bed. He had never been with someone who didn't expect to get off right away, didn't expect to receive everything he gave tit for tat. But he had learned Spencer was a uniquely generous lover, seeming to get pleasure from making Emilio feel good and not expecting anything in return. Not that it stopped Emilio from trying to give as good as he got. Hell, nothing made him hotter than watching Spencer come apart under his ministrations.

"I love you," Spencer mumbled against Emilio's mouth. He dropped another soft kiss on Emilio's lips and then rested his head on Emilio's shoulder, wiggling until they were even closer together, with nothing but Spencer's underwear separating them, and held on tightly.

With the fog of passion finally lifting, Emilio took stock of their position. They were sitting on the floor just inside the bedroom, Spencer was wearing only briefs, with the rest of his clothes in a heap next to them, and Emilio's shirt was rucked up his chest and his pants tangled around his knees. The situation made him chuckle.

"What?" Spencer asked, raising his head and looking at Emilio.

"Look at us." Emilio nudged his chin at their bodies. "We're on the floor and I've still got all my clothes on."

Spencer looked over his shoulder and then smiled at Emilio. "I think it's sort of hot," he said.

"Hot?"

"I don't know." Spencer kissed the side of Emilio's neck. "It's like we were so into each other we couldn't wait to get in bed or take all our clothes off or..." He let the words trail off and shrugged. "Hot."

"Yeah, well, you said you wanted to get me off. That kind of makes my brain short out and all I can think about is making contact between my dick and your body."

Spencer dropped his hand to Emilio's exposed package. "Technically, you accomplished your goal." Then he tugged on his T-shirt. "But just barely."

"I'm only getting started," Emilio said. "How about you?" He rubbed his palm over Spencer's cloth-covered erection, making him tremble. "What do you want?"

Spencer peppered kisses along Emilio's neck and jaw. "I want you to top me," he said. "Is that okay?"

"Okay?" Emilio chuckled. "Making love to you is one of my favorite things in life." He dropped his hands down the back of Spencer's briefs and fondled his ass. "Just give me a minute to recover." He caressed Spencer's back and held him close, enjoying the feeling of Spencer's breath ghosting over his neck and the clean scent of his hair. "You know, this is one of my other favorite things," Emilio said. "Cuddling with you."

"I love that you say things like that." Spencer moved his hand under Emilio's shirt and traced his nipple with one finger. "And I love it too."

"Cuddling?" Emilio asked.

"Yes." Spencer shifted until their gazes met. "And feeling you inside me." Spencer's eyes looked shiny and his voice hitched. "I missed that so much," he said. "When we first got together I think I told you I like to bottom, but the truth is, for a long time, I've been scared I'd never really be able to like it again. But now...with you." He swallowed hard. "It's even better than it was before... It's amazing." He brushed Emilio's hair back off his face. "You're amazing." Spencer blinked and smiled ruefully. "And I am sappy as all get-out. Quick, say something to save us from going into a sugar coma!"

"Oh, uh, okay." Emilio rubbed his lips together and furrowed his brow in thought. "Wanna fuck?"

"Nice," Spencer said with a laugh.

"No, seriously." Emilio grasped Spencer's hand and led it to his hard dick. "What you said got me revved up all over again."

"Nice," Spencer said, his voice husky that time. "I'll remember to be sappy more often."

"Or naked," Emilio suggested. "Naked is good too."

Spencer climbed off Emilio's lap, hooked his thumbs in his briefs and pushed them to his ankles, putting a little wiggle into it. Then he leaned down, brushed his lips over Emilio's, and whispered, "Take me to bed."

Emilio scrambled up and yanked on his shirt, almost falling in the process. "Damn it," he grumbled as he pulled the shirt over his head. His jeans had twisted around his legs and gotten caught under his shoe so it took some maneuvering to get the whole mess off. Finally, he was able to push all of his clothes to his bare feet and kick them away. "There," he said breathlessly, planting his hands on his hips and looking up.

Spencer was watching him, his lips pressed together and his entire body shaking, like he was holding in laughter.

Thinking of how ridiculous his entire undressing process must have looked, Emilio chuckled and said, "I see you enjoyed my sexy striptease."

"I really, really did," Spencer responded, stepping close and wrapping his arms around Emilio's waist.

"Oh, yeah? What did it for you the most? Was it the part where I almost fell on my ass? Or the part where my dick flopped around?"

"Um, hard to say," Spencer answered. "I think it was the whole thing."

"Right," Emilio said with a laugh. He dropped a kiss on Spencer's forehead. "Now that I've gotten you all worked up with my suave moves, can we go to bed?"

"Yes." Spencer walked over to the bed and started crawling onto it, but stopped when he heard Emilio's loud groan. "What?" he asked, looking back over his shoulder.

Emilio dragged his gaze from Spencer's ass to his face. "Love this fuckin' view," he said as he wrapped his hand around his shaft and started stroking.

"Come and get it, then," Spencer said, shaking that tight

ass.

Emilio laughed and jumped onto the bed. He grasped Spencer's hips and held him steady as he buried his face in Spencer's gorgeous butt, nipping and licking.

Spencer moaned and tucked his knees underneath him, rocking back against Emilio's face. "Want you," he rasped as he reached for the lube. He rolled onto his back and handed it to Emilio, his eyes full of trust.

Emilio took the bottle from Spencer and coated his fingers with slick before tossing it aside. "I want you too," he said. "So damn much." He knelt between Spencer's legs and stroked his finger up and down his crease, eventually circling his hole and pressing inside.

Spencer raised his hips and moaned.

"Feel good?" Emilio asked as he moved his finger in and out of Spencer's body.

"Yes." Spencer looked into Emilio's eyes and reached for him. "I want more." He spread his legs on top of Emilio's thighs.

Emilio rubbed his hand over his own dick, coating it with lube, then planted one hand on the bed and moved himself into position, pressing his crown against Spencer's puckered opening. "You ready for me?" he asked.

"Always," Spencer said.

Emilio slowly pressed inside, reveling in the feeling of tightness and silky heat surrounding him.

"Love this," Spencer whispered once Emilio was fully

seated. "Love you."

Emilio smiled down at him. "Love you too," he said, dipping down and rubbing the tip of his nose against Spencer's.

Spencer's eyes twinkled as he gazed up at him. He was smiling widely, completely free of any tension or fear. And Emilio knew that whatever else he did in his life, he'd make sure to keep that expression on Spencer's face. Always.

# EPILOGUE

"HEY, SLEEPYHEAD. Time to wake up."

"Mnph," Spencer grunted, reached for his pillow, and flopped it on top of his head.

"Goddamn, you're cute." Emilio's happy voice penetrated the pillow. "But you still gotta wake up."

Spencer peered out from underneath the fabric. "It's Sunday."

"Uh-huh." Emilio spread out on the bed next to him, picked the pillow up, and kissed Spencer's head.

"We can sleep in on Sundays," Spencer reminded him.

"It's ten o'clock," Emilio said. "We did sleep in."

"We just went to sleep a few hours ago," Spencer whined. He flicked his eyes over Emilio's body. "Why are you dressed?"

Emilio rolled on top of him and tugged his lower lip between both of his. "We went to sleep at eleven," he reminded Spencer.

"But then you woke me up." Spencer stretched his neck and kissed Emilio.

"I don't remember you complaining," Emilio said huskily.

"And besides, you're the one who woke me up."

Spencer's lips curled up in a smile. "That was the third time. You woke me up the first two times."

"Yeah, I guess I did." Emilio grinned down at him. "Are you awake now?"

"Yes," Spencer admitted reluctantly.

"Good." Emilio bounced off the bed and held his hand out. "Let's go."

Spencer scooted his face to the edge of the bed right in front of Emilio. With Emilio standing and Spencer on his hands and knees, he was at the perfect height for optimal access to Emilio's groin, so he started mouthing that thick dick through the denim. "You sure you don't want to come back to bed?"

Emilio groaned and reached for Spencer's head, then he stopped and stepped back. "No time," he said, sounding a little out of breath.

"Spoilsport." Spencer sat up and stuck his tongue out.

"Oh, now *that* is adorable." Emilio leaned in and licked his tongue. "But it isn't going to distract me. Let's go."

"Fine," Spencer sighed dramatically and walked over to the pile of clothes he had worn the day before. Four months into the remodeling project, Emilio had the electrical work, bathroom, and painting done, and the kitchen almost ready for use. The floors were the last big job, and he had been working on them all week. Spencer had spent Saturday helping him as best he could. "The floors await. Let's do it."

"I finished the floors this morning."

"You did?" Spencer halted and looked at Emilio in surprise.

"Yup. We were pretty much done last night. I just needed to wait for everything to dry so I could mop on another coat of finish in the living room." Emilio walked over and swatted Spencer's backside. "You have enough time for a shower, but then we need to get going."

"Are you saying I smell bad?" Spencer scowled and crossed his arms over his chest, pretending to be mad.

"I'm saying you smell like spunk." Emilio raised his eyebrows. "Ain't nothing bad about that, but I figured you wouldn't wanna see my mother that way."

Spencer looked down and rubbed his hand over his belly, encountering a crusty reminder of the previous night. Heat rose up his neck as he thought about how hard he had screamed when he had made that particular mess. He had been on his back with Emilio on top of him, holding his legs wide open and slamming inside over and over again.

"Wait!" Spencer jerked, Emilio's words finally penetrating his foggy brain. "Did you say something about your mother?"

"Yup." Emilio sauntered over and took Spencer's elbow, leading him out of the bedroom and into the remodeled bathroom. "We're gonna have lunch with my parents, so we gotta hurry."

"We are?" Spencer shook his head, trying to clear away all remnants of sleep.

"Yeah." Emilio turned the shiny platinum shower handle and then held the glass door open for Spencer.

"I don't remember talking about this." He stepped into the shower and, as he did every morning, admired the white marble penny tiles Emilio had laid over the ceiling, walls, and floor.

"That's because I didn't tell you," Emilio explained as he clicked the door closed.

Spencer's jaw dropped, and he flipped around, staring at Emilio through the glass. "You intentionally kept this from me?"

"Yup." Emilio nodded and waved his hand toward the water. "Gotta hurry, Spence. We don't want to be late."

Spencer ducked his head under the showerhead and then reached for the shampoo. "I can't believe you didn't tell me." He lathered his hair. "Why would you do something like that?"

"Because every time we go to my parents' house, you spend at least three days before fretting about it."

"I don't fret," Spencer said stubbornly. He leaned back, started to rinse the shampoo, and jolted when he realized there wouldn't be time to make anything. "Emi—"

"Nobody else brings food," Emilio said, correctly predicting his concern. "Finish rinsing your hair."

Spencer grumbled but rinsed the shampoo out. It wasn't the first time Emilio had said they weren't expected to bring anything when they visited his family, but Spencer resolutely refused to arrive empty-handed, so he always made sure to make a side dish or a dessert anyway. He scrubbed his body hurriedly, turned off the water, and yanked the door open. Emilio was waiting for him with a towel.

"I just need fifteen minutes and I can make..." He stopped midsentence when he remembered the state of their kitchen. Emilio had installed the new cabinets and appliances a week earlier, and they were waiting for the countertops to arrive on Tuesday. Until then, every kitchen utensil and the entire contents of the pantry were packed away in boxes.

Just when Spencer was about to go into full-scale panic, Emilio wrapped the towel around him and said, "I ran out this morning and bought brownies from that fancy bakery down the street." He kissed Spencer's cheek and then dried his hair. "Everyone loves brownies."

"You did?" Spencer looked up at him in relief.

"Yeah, I did." He cupped Spencer's cheek. "But I'm telling you we really don't gotta do that. Nobody expects us to bring something every time we come over."

"I know." Spencer ducked his chin and rubbed his toe back and forth over the soft bath mat. "I just want them to like me."

"Ah, *cariño*." Emilio kissed him gently. "My family loves you. My brothers think it's great you can teach them that angle shit to help with pool, my sister wants to be your best friend, my mother won't stop feeding you, and my father has taken to doing math problems he finds on the Internet and showing you how he solved them. You gotta stop worrying."

"I'll try," Spencer promised.

"Good." Emilio kissed him again, then hung up the towel and tugged Spencer out of the bathroom.

"But you got brownies, right?" Spencer asked.

Emilio laughed, so Spencer pinched his ass.

"Hey!" Emilio shouted, rubbing his hand over the injured area. "Right, right! I got brownies."

Spencer laughed and walked over to the bedroom. He opened the closet, pulled out his underwear drawer, and froze.

"You like them?" Emilio asked from behind him.

Spencer ran his hand over the pile of brightly colored fabric and landed on a bright-blue pair. He picked it up and looked back over his shoulder.

"That one's my favorite," Emilio said huskily. "Check out the back."

He looked down at the new underwear, skimmed his finger over the mesh cloth, and flipped it over. Then he jerked his head up and twisted around, looking at Emilio again. "There is no back," he pointed out.

"Exactly." Emilio's voice held that wicked tone that always ramped Spencer right up. He reverently caressed Spencer's backside. "An ass as fine as yours shouldn't be covered up." He pressed his front to Spencer's back and whispered in his ear, "You said you'd wear these for me, remember?" Emilio took the underwear from Spencer's hand

and squatted, holding it out.

Spencer turned around and looked down, meeting Emilio's heated gaze. "That was months ago," he said thickly as he stepped into the jock.

"Mmm hmm." Emilio looked up and licked his lips. "I told you I wouldn't forget." He stood slowly, pulling the jock up Spencer's legs. Already throbbing with need, Spencer whimpered when Emilio reached down and adjusted his hard dick. "There you go, *cariño*," Emilio said, patting Spencer's package. "You can put your pants and shirt on now."

With shaky hands, Spencer pulled a polo shirt out of the closet, dropped it over his head, and stepped into his pants. "I'm going to be hard all day now," he said as he slipped on his shoes. Not that he was complaining. He loved that feeling.

"Yeah, you are," Emilio said, looking at him knowingly. "But I promise to take good care of you and your fine ass as soon as we get home."

"Okay." Spencer nodded, then glanced at Emilio and turned one side of his lips up. "Hey, since nothing's covered up back there"—he stepped over to Emilio and circled his hips against him—"can I keep these on while you do it?"

"Jesus." Emilio bucked and reached down for Spencer's ass.

"Time to go," Spencer said as he danced away. "We don't want to be late." Then he strutted out of the room, putting an extra sway in his step.

"You're gonna kill me," Emilio muttered from behind

him as they walked down the hallway.

"No dying until you bend me over and top me hard enough for us to find out if the mesh on this underwear holds my cum."

He heard Emilio gasp, followed by a thumping sound. "I'm okay," Emilio said, sounding frazzled. "Just tripped."

Spencer laughed all the way to the car.

EMILIO TURNED onto his parents' street and started counting silently. He had gotten to three when Spencer said, "Emilio?"

"Yeah."

"Do you know why there are so many cars here today?"

"Yup. It's my parents' turn to host the Alonso family Christmas party." He tried to keep his voice calm and soothing.

"Who is the Alonso family?" Spencer asked, sounding a little nervous, but not anywhere near the way he used to get when they visited Emilio's parents.

"My *abuela* on my mother's side was an Alonso. Most of that generation has passed, but their kids decided to carry on the tradition, so they take turns hosting a big family party the Sunday before Christmas every other year. Between my mom's siblings and her cousins, there are so many people on the list nobody'll have to do it more than once, so it ain't a lot of trouble."

Spencer was quiet as Emilio pulled into his parents' driveway and parked behind their car. "And I gather you didn't mention this because you didn't want me to worry?"

"Yup." Emilio took the keys out of the ignition.

"So how many people will be here?" Spencer asked.

"I don't know exactly. It's different every year." Emilio twisted to the side and took Spencer's hand in his. "But I'll be with you the whole time, okay? You're gonna be fine."

"I know." Spencer smiled weakly. "I'm a little nervous, but I love your family. And you don't need to babysit me. I know how to mingle and make small talk." He took a deep breath and opened the car door. "Let's go."

EVEN WITH a house and yard full of people, they ended up spending most of the day hanging out with Emilio's brothers and sister. By early evening, they were in the front room, stuffed on a love seat with Henry, the rest of the furniture and most of the floor space occupied by Emilio's siblings and their spouses, and his father sitting in his ratty armchair regaling them with embarrassing childhood stories while his mother handed distant relatives plates of leftovers as they left.

"Oh, Carmen, wait just one minute," Emilio's mother said

to a woman who looked vaguely familiar. "I have more of those olives you liked. I'll just put them in a box." She hurried away, leaving Carmen and the two men she was with waiting by the door.

"Nice to see you, Carmen," Emilio's father said from his armchair. "I'm sorry we didn't get to catch up."

He started to get up but Carmen waved her hand and said, "No, no, you sit. You must be tired after such a long day. Alejandro had to work today and Lucia moved to Tucson, but you remember my son Adan." She pointed to one of the men and completely disregarded the other.

"Sure, sure," Emilio's father said. "Good to see you again."

Adan's lips were pursed in what looked to be frustration. "Good to see you too, Mr. Sanchez. Thank you for hosting the party." He stepped closer to the man next to him and put his hand on his shoulder. "This is"—Carmen cleared her throat loudly, and Adan flinched—"my roommate, Scott Boone."

"How nice that you were able to come to the party," Emilio's father said. "How long have you two been together?" Carmen gasped, clearly not expecting the comment, and Adan looked like he had swallowed his tongue. Completely oblivious to the reaction to his innocent question, Emilio's father continued speaking. "Oh! You boys must know my son Emilio and his boyfriend Spencer. They're gay too."

Scott snorted out a laugh and then looked down at his feet, his shoulders shaking.

"Uh, no," Adan said. "It's not really—"

"Adan, let's go," Carmen snapped as she swung the door open. "Thank you for a lovely afternoon," she called back over her shoulder as she stormed out of the house, her son stomping after her.

"Hey, I'll see you guys at the next club meeting," Scott said, giving Emilio and Spencer a wink as he walked out the door and closed it behind him, drowning out Carmen's rising voice.

The room was quiet for a few beats, and then everybody erupted in laughter.

"What?" Emilio's father asked, looking at his children in confusion. "What's so funny?"

Henry rolled off the love seat and held his belly as he gasped for air. "Hey, Emilio, man, what do you guys do at those club meetings?"

"Shut up," Emilio said as he laughed.

"I saw a thing on the Internet once," Henry said.

"Henry," Martin said, the warning clear in his tone. "We are in mixed company."

"Right, right. I got it." Henry held his hand up and nodded as he climbed back onto the couch. "But just tell me this, 'Milio. Do you guys gotta wear flip-flops at the meetings so you don't slip on the—"

Emilio shoved Henry off the couch at the same time Raul and Martin both shouted, "Henry!"

"Why would they need flip-flops?" Emilio's father asked in confusion. "Are your meetings at the pool?"

Spencer started coughing uncontrollably, and Emilio patted him on the back. "We don't got meetings, Pop. Henry's just messing around."

"Oh. Well you should. Meetings are important. I'm sure your mother would be happy to make her special empanadas, and Spencer could make those lemon bars he brought over last week." He paused and looked at Spencer. "Do you have any more of those lemon bars?"

"No, sir," Spencer said, sounding a little breathless from all the laughter. "But I can make more and bring them over next weekend."

"DID YOU have fun today?" Emilio asked Spencer when they got home.

"I did." Spencer bobbed his head. "Everyone was really nice, Henry is hilarious, and your mom kept trying to feed me."

"Well, she can't have one of her boys walking around looking skinny," Emilio said, repeating his mother's words. "People will think she doesn't know how to cook." Spencer had lit up when he had heard Emilio's mother make the comment, looking so pleased that he was considered part of the family.

"I'm not skinny," Spencer said, ducking his head and

blushing.

"No?" Emilio asked. "Let me check." He rushed forward and goosed Spencer.

"Ack!" Spencer screeched and jumped.

"Hmm, I don't know. I better check again." Emilio reached for Spencer, but he dodged him and ran down the hallway.

"C'mere," Emilio said, chasing after him. "It's for science!"

When they got to the bedroom, Emilio wrapped his arms around Spencer's waist and tumbled them onto the bed together.

"Emilio!" Spencer shouted.

"Yeah?" Emilio asked as he shoved both hands down the back of Spencer's pants and started massaging his bare globes.

Spencer's breath hitched.

"Mmm, these don't feel skinny to me, *cariño*." Emilio dragged a finger down Spencer's trench before going back to his cheeks and squeezing them. "I think they're firm and round and just right."

"You...you do?" Spencer stuttered as he arched into Emilio's touch. "Maybe you should take a closer look." He gulped. "Just to be sure."

"Good idea," Emilio whispered into his ear. "I like how you think." He reached for Spencer's shirt first, tugged it up, and pulled it over his head. Then he scooted down and took off Spencer's shoes, socks, and finally his pants, leaving him wearing only the blue jock. "Damn." Emilio's voice shook as he looked at the beautiful man sharing his bed. He pressed the heel of his hand over his dick. "You make me need so much, Spence." He locked his gaze with Spencer's. "So much."

"Me too," Spencer said hoarsely. "Kiss me?"

"Always." Emilio lowered himself on top of Spencer and pressed their lips together, enjoying gentle kisses and soft touches.

"Off," Spencer said as he shoved Emilio's shirt up his back.

Emilio planted his hands on the bed and straightened his arms, giving Spencer room to pull the shirt over his head. Then he lifted one arm at a time and threw the garment off the bed.

"Now your pants," Spencer said.

"Your wish is my command." Emilio grinned as he toed off his shoes and socks and wiggled out of his jeans. "Good?" he asked.

"Almost." Spencer took hold of Emilio's briefs and shoved them down his legs, using his foot to get them all the way off. "Okay, now we're ready."

"Ready for what?" Emilio asked, trying to look innocent. "Are we going to one of those club meetings with Adam and Scott?"

"Adan," Spencer corrected him. "He's your cousin. Shouldn't you know his name?"

"He's a second cousin a hundred times removed or some shit. That was probably the first time I've seen him in my life."

"That's too bad," Spencer said quietly. "Because I bet he'd really like knowing he has family members as wonderful as yours. I didn't get the impression his mother was particularly supportive."

Emilio knew Spencer related to that situation all too well. "You know, we can go spend Christmas with your family, if you want. If we go online, I bet we can find last-minute flights."

"Why would we do that?" Spencer asked, looking horrified. "Everyone's going to your parents' house. I'm helping your mother bake the ham. She asked me specifically."

"Yeah, I know she did." Emilio grinned. "She thinks you're a great cook." He brushed his hand through Spencer's hair. "I just wanted to make sure I wasn't keeping you from your family."

Spencer dropped his gaze and quietly said, "Would it sound horrible if I told you that your parents and siblings feel more like family to me than mine has in a very long time?"

Emilio's chest tightened. "I'm sad you don't feel connected to your parents and your brother, Spence, but you're a part of my family now, so no, it don't sound horrible to hear that you feel that way." He tilted Spencer's chin up. "I ain't met your folks, so I don't know what their deal is, but you're ours now. We want you and we ain't gonna let you go."

"Promise?" Spencer asked.

"I do." Emilio nodded. "Easiest promise I ever made."

"Emilio?" Spencer said softly as he trailed his fingers

over Emilio's hand.

"Yeah?"

"If I got you a ring, would you wear it?"

Emilio's heart sped up. "What kind of ring?" he asked.

"Whatever kind you want," Spencer answered. "I was just thinking if you wore it here"—he traced the ring finger on Emilio's left hand—"everyone would know you were taken." He glanced up at Emilio, looking nervous but hopeful.

"Yeah, *cariño*," Emilio answered thickly. "If you got me a ring like that, I'd wear it."

Spencer smiled, then dipped his head and kissed Emilio's hand.

"Spence?" Emilio said.

"Uh-huh." Spencer rubbed his cheek over Emilio's hand.

"If I get you a ring, will you wear it?"

Spencer gulped and looked up at Emilio. "What kind of ring?" he asked hoarsely.

"Whatever kind you want. But you gotta wear it here—" Emilio brought Spencer's left hand to his mouth and swirled his tongue around Spencer's ring finger before sucking it between his lips. "So everyone knows you belong to me."

Spencer trembled. "Yes," he gasped. "If you get me a ring like that, I'll wear it forever."

They gazed at each other for several long seconds, and Emilio absorbed the commitment they'd just made. Deciding it was the best moment of his life, he wrapped Spencer in his arms and held him closely, never wanting to let go.

"Do you have plans after work tomorrow?" Spencer asked.

"No." Emilio shook his head. "What do you have in mind?"

"Well," Spencer said, drawing out the word, "I was thinking we could go ring shopping."

Emilio smiled so broadly his cheeks hurt. He pressed his lips to Spencer's and mumbled, "Let's go ring shopping, *cariño.*"

## THE END

# ABOUT THE AUTHOR

Cardeno C.—CC to friends—is a hopeless romantic who wants to add a lot of happiness and a few *awwws* into a reader's day. Writing is a nice break from real life as a corporate type and volunteer work with gay rights organizations. Cardeno's stories range from sweet to intense, contemporary to paranormal, long to short, but they always include strong relationships and walks into the happily-ever-after sunset.

Email: cardenoc@gmail.com

Website: www.cardenoc.com

Twitter: https://twitter.com/cardenoc

Facebook: http://www.facebook.com/CardenoC

Pinterest: http://www.pinterest.com/cardenoC

Blog: http://caferisque.blogspot.com

# OTHER BOOKS BY CARDENO C.

# AVAILABLE NOW

## The Half of Us

*If short-tempered Jason can open his heart and life to optimistic*
*Abe, he might finally find the family he craves.*

Short-tempered, arrogant heart surgeon Jason Garcia grew up wanting a close-knit family, but believes he ruined those dreams when he broke up his marriage. The benefit of divorce is having as much random sex as he wants, and it's a benefit Jason is exploiting when he meets a sweet, shy man at a bar and convinces him to go home for a no-strings-attached night of fun.

Eight years living in Las Vegas hasn't dimmed Abe Green's optimism, earnestness, or desire to find the one. When a sexy man with lonely eyes propositions him, Abe decides to give himself a birthday present—one night of spontaneous fun with no thoughts of the future. But one night turns into two and then three, and Abe realizes his heart is involved.

For the first time, Abe feels safe enough with someone he respects and adores to let go of his inhibitions in the bedroom. If Jason can get past his own inhibitions and open his heart and his life to Abe, he might finally find the family he craves.

## Something in the Way He Needs

*Controlled Asher didn't expect to fall for free-spirited Daniel, but*
*they'll find what they desperately need in one another.*

Police captain Asher Penaz's staunch professionalism bleeds into his home life, down to his neatly pressed attire and spartan apartment. He enjoys being in charge and in control, so his sudden and powerful attraction to the lighthearted, free-spirited Daniel Tover throws him for a loop. In his entire life, Daniel has never gotten what he needs, so he moves to the next place, the next job, the next attempt to find something worth staying for, always landing at the top of his game, but never feeling like he belongs.

The chemistry between Asher and Daniel sizzles, but with all that fire comes the risk of getting burned. As both men struggle to learn themselves while getting to know each other, the lines of desire and control blur. If Daniel and Asher can walk through the flames together, they might find what they desperately need.

## More than Everything

*Time might not heal all wounds, but with two motivated and strong-willed men on a campaign to win him back, Charlie will get more than he ever thought possible.*

As a teenager, Charlie "Chase" Rhodes meets Scott Boone and falls head over heels in love with the popular, athletic boy next door. Charlie thinks he's living the dream when Scott says he feels the same way. But his dreams are dashed when Scott unexpectedly moves away.

Years later, Charlie meets brash and confident Adan Navarro, who claims all he wants is a round between the sheets. After eight months together, Charlie is convinced Adan returns his love. But when the opportunity comes to be open about their relationship, Adan walks away.

Time passes and life moves on, but when Charlie learns the only two men he's ever loved are now in love with each other, his heart breaks all over again. Scott and Adan tell Charlie they want him back, but Charlie doesn't know if he can trust two people who have hurt him so deeply. Time might not heal all wounds, but with two motivated and strong-willed men on a campaign to win him back, Charlie will get more than he ever thought possible.

## Walk With Me

*Serious, responsible Seth longs for sexy, outspoken Eli but must decide if he's willing to veer from his safe life-plan.*

When Eli Block steps into his parents' living room and sees his childhood crush sitting on the couch, he starts a shameless campaign to seduce the young rabbi. Unfortunately, Seth Cohen barely remembers Eli and he resolutely shuts down all his advances. As a tenuous and then binding friendship forms between the two men, Eli must find a way to move past his unrequited love while still keeping his best friend in his life. Not an easy feat when the same person occupies both roles.

Professional, proper Seth is shocked by Eli's brashness, overt sexuality, and easy defiance of societal norms. But he's also drawn to the happy, funny, light-filled man. As their friendship